SKELETONS IN THE ATTIC

David Schutte was born in Crouch End, North London. Brain surgeon, pop singer and Olympic athlete are just some of the things he never achieved. Apart from being an author, he is also a specialist children's bookseller. He lives in Hampshire with his wife and children.

DAVID SCHUTTE

SKELETONS
IN THE ATTIC

To Thomas

Best wishes

David Schutte

Junior Genius

First published in 2001 by Junior Genius
93 Milford Hill, Salisbury, Wiltshire SP1 2QL

ISBN 1-904028-04-7

Copyright © David Schutte 2001

1 3 5 7 9 8 6 4 2

A CIP catalogue record for this book
is available from the British Library

Printed in the U.K. by
Polestar AUP Aberdeen Ltd

TO

my big brother TOM

who led us into adventure

Contents

1.	Birthday Present	9
2.	In the Attic	20
3.	Birthday Past	27
4.	Runaway Joe	35
5.	The Man in the Green Sports Car	44
6.	The Man on the Telephone	55
7.	Certificates	66
8.	Invitation	78
9.	Passmeadow Hall	90
10.	The Meeting	96
11.	Fly Away, Peter	105
12.	Hunted	111
13.	The Letter	122
14.	In the Churchyard	129
15.	Eckington Bridge	137
16.	Journey's End	146

CHAPTER ONE

Birthday Present

If it was dark enough, and if it was quiet enough, Peter could hear the voice in his head. Sometimes he stayed awake on purpose until the world had gone to sleep, just to listen.

He was listening now. It was pitch black except for a splash of pale yellow light that spilled under his door from the hall. And it was silent, except for the comforting tick of the grandfather clock downstairs, and the regular rhythm of his uncle snoring in the next bedroom.

He had first heard the voice when he was little, maybe three or four years old. His mother always told him it was ghosts, and that he should never listen to ghosts. Then, before he was seven, with no warning, it had stopped.

It had returned once when he was nine. He remembered the sky was black that night, and moonless. There was an electricity cut, so there was no background hum of fridges or motors, and no street lights glowing yellow on his curtains. His oil lamp had gone out, it was late, and there had been no traffic for a while. In this black silence, he had heard it again, thin, like the distant piping of a flute from a far country. It lasted for only a few minutes. It was blotted out when a selfish driver revved his engine in the road outside, screeched his tyres and roared away into the darkness past his window.

Now the voice had come back again. He'd first noticed its return ten weeks ago – a month before his mother had died. He'd heard it almost every night since then – when it was dark and quiet enough, and as long as he stayed awake until after eleven.

The clock ticked, and his uncle stopped snoring.

Soon, it arrived. It bumped into his mind like a demented moth attacking a light bulb, nudging his brain, trying frantically to tell him something.

But he never knew what it was saying. It was like Joe's mother talking to him when he was at Joe's house trying to watch television. He'd hear her speaking, and he'd say "Yes" automatically, even though he hadn't a clue what she'd said. That's what the voice was like, only he couldn't understand it even when he tried to listen. It seemed to be calling *him*, yet it didn't seem to know his name.

This time the sound of fighting cats suddenly erupted in the distance. The voice was gone in an instant, startled like a bird at the sound of a gunshot.

Peter lay awake a little longer, wondering if it would come back . . .

Presently, his thoughts wandered to the following day. Like all the forty-two days since his mother had died, he wasn't looking forward to it much. Not a single day had been happy since then. When the unimaginable had happened, his uncle Len had stepped in as his guardian. It was in his mother's will.

Like her letter.

He'd never understood her letter. The solicitor had given it to him when no one else was looking. For him. From his mother. It was under the pillow now, where he kept it at night. He groped for it with the ends of his fingers and felt comforted. It was safe. During the day he kept it inside his shirt. He didn't want anyone else to read it, ever. He thought of his poor mother . . . Saw her face, now, felt tears swelling against the pillow, soaking in.

He'd never liked his sour-faced uncle, and it hadn't taken long for Peter to discover what he was like to live with. But there was no one else. His aunt in Canada had died, and so had his mother's parents, before he was born. And he'd never known his father.

Peter listened to his uncle's snoring now, starting again in unison with the clock. Four ticks to one snore. Loud and vulgar – like his voice when he was awake. At least when his uncle was asleep he was out of sight, Peter thought. He had soon grown used to the bubbling snore, but wondered if he would ever get used to living with its owner during the hours of daylight. He wished his uncle wouldn't keep moaning and carping, picking holes in everything he did.

He tried not to think about it, turning his thoughts instead to the brown paper parcel he had seen his uncle bring home the previous day. It was Peter's birthday soon. Half of him hoped – for no logical reason – that the brown paper parcel was a present. The other half couldn't believe it. His uncle had never gone out of his way to buy him anything. He'd never given him anything since he'd known him. Peter even had to ask for his pocket money each week. His uncle never handed it over unless Peter asked for it. It was as if he actually enjoyed Peter's discomfort.

His mother . . . His mother had always given him his pocket money before he'd thought of it himself . . .

All the same, he wanted to know about the parcel. As soon as his uncle had gone to work, he'd get his friend Joe round. They'd see if they could find it and look inside . . .

The voice didn't come again that night. Peter slept.

At eight-fifteen the following morning, a man in a light green sports car pulled in to the kerb opposite number thirty-four, Ford Avenue. Turning his head slowly, he counted along the houses.

"Thirty-four, thirty-two, thirty, *twenty-eight*." Darting blue eyes, squinting behind rimless glasses, came to rest on number twenty-eight. The man looked up and down the net-curtained windows, then glanced at the piece of paper that

11

lay on the seat beside him. Carefully written in large, neat letters, it said:

> *Mrs Caroline Turner*
> *28, Ford Avenue*

and underneath:

> *(Miss Deirdre Briscoe??)*

The man turned off the engine and sat still, staring at the blank windows, thinking. He picked up the morning's newspaper and started thumbing the pages. Every now and again he stopped reading and glanced in the direction of the house. If anyone walked along the road, or if any vehicles slowed down, he watched them, checking to see if they might call at number twenty-eight. None of them did.

At a quarter to nine the front door of the house began to open.

Peter closed the front door again. He thought he'd heard Joe coming up the path, but there was no sign of anyone. He hovered by the window in the hall, watching. A light green sports car was parked three houses away, one he hadn't seen before. The driver was still in it, pretending to read. Peter knew he was pretending, because every few seconds he looked up from the newspaper and glanced towards Peter's house. Peter tried to see the number plate, but it was hidden by the car in front.

Then his uncle came down the stairs. He stood in front of the hall mirror, turning his face from side to side, tilting his head back, admiring himself.

Peter looked on with distaste. He couldn't help it. He stared at his uncle's weak chin, protruding yellow teeth, crinkly black hair. Cold eyes stared through a pair of glasses like dead-fish eyes.

The sour expression on his uncle's face didn't flicker as he noticed Peter watching him through the mirror.

"Going to waste the whole day doing nothing, as usual?" he said. He straightened his new tie and brushed hairs off his new suit. His voice had its usual tone – flat, without emotion.

Peter tried not to meet the lifeless stare. Lowering his eyes, he moved away from the window.

"Don't know."

His uncle picked up his new briefcase and jangled car keys in his hand – keys of the brand new executive model he'd bought a few weeks after Peter's mother had died. Peter wondered how he'd got so much money so suddenly. Before, he'd lived in a council flat and driven a rusty old banger.

"I've got important people coming here for a meeting tonight," his uncle was saying. He always pronounced his words syllable by syllable, as if he was dictating to a first-generation computer. "So make yourself unobtrusive, right?"

Peter shrugged. He didn't know what unobtrusive meant, but he could guess. Get lost.

"And don't leave remnants of your meals all over the kitchen or dirty dishes in the sink like you usually do. I want this place clean when I get in. And don't play any of your stupid music when they're here."

Peter shrugged again.

"Okay."

He watched his uncle open the front door and stride towards his new car looking pompous – probably hoping the neighbours were watching. His head nodded slowly from side to side as if he was someone important, or as if his brain was so heavy it was awkward to balance.

Peter went to the front door and closed it. He felt the same

13

wave of relief and freedom that flowed over him every time his uncle left the house.

He thought how different it had been when his mother was alive . . . She would give him a nice smile, put a cool hand on the side of his face, kiss his forehead. It had always made him feel good. He wouldn't have wanted his school friends to see, but he'd secretly enjoyed the sudden immersion in her thick cloying perfume – looked forward to her coming home again at lunch-time and in the evening, often with cakes or chocolate bars. Looked forward to her jokes and her fun . . .

His uncle never brought him anything.

Peter felt a stab of pain, and quickly pushed the thoughts aside before they could hurt him again. They had hurt him too many times in the six weeks since she'd gone.

He forced his attention away from the horrible ache, back to the brown paper parcel. Lifted the net curtain to make sure his uncle was really going. His uncle didn't see him. He was already in his new fantasy business world, pretending he was someone special, preening himself with dreams of success and making lots of money. Even Peter, not yet thirteen, knew the truth. He couldn't believe that anyone else could be fooled. But they were. Tonight's visitors must have been fooled, otherwise they wouldn't be coming.

He watched the car slide backwards from the drive, slowly enough for the neighbours to notice, pause in the road, then surge into the distance.

He followed it almost out of sight, then glanced along the pavement in the opposite direction, wondering if Joe would come. The light green sports car was still there. It was a classic, just the sort his mother had always fancied. He wished he could have bought it for her . . .

Even as he pushed the hurting thought away, the driver started the car's engine, slapped it into gear and sped off in the same direction as his uncle. It was almost as if he'd been waiting to follow him. Peter's suspicions were roused even further. He tried to memorise what the man looked like. A bit chubby with a moustache; middle-aged; spectacles; as bald as a brick. He forgot to look at the number plate as it passed.

Peter wondered who he was, and what he wanted.

There weren't many cupboards in the house. Peter decided to start with the one under the stairs. He'd just taken out some tools and old pots of paint when the front doorbell rang.

He panicked. It was probably nosy old Mrs Spinks, his nutty next-door neighbour. He pushed everything back in place and closed the cupboard door, hoping that she hadn't been looking through the letterbox. She always told his uncle everything, whether he wanted to hear it or not.

He went to the front door, his face red with effort. He was relieved to find Joe – tall, thin, fair-haired, grinning.

"You look guilty," said Joe, stepping inside. "You'd be no good as a criminal."

Peter whistled a two-tone sigh as he moved to one side to let his friend pass.

"Uncle Len brought something home last night," he said, wasting no time. "A parcel. It might be a birthday present. Do you want to help me look for it?"

"You bet!"

Peter drew the curtain across the front door this time, so that no one – namely, Mrs Spinks – could spy through the letterbox. Meanwhile, Joe had dived under the stairs and emerged with a Russian hat on. It belonged to Peter's uncle. It covered half Joe's head, and the only parts left showing were the tip of Joe's nose and a big grin. Peter laughed.

"Stay there!" said Joe. He disappeared into the cupboard again and came out wearing a white raincoat. It trailed on the floor, enveloping him completely. Encouraged by

15

Peter's laughter, he took a step forward, showing off like a fashion model. He twirled round, tripped on the coat hem, and fell clumsily on to the hall table. Table and telephone went in opposite directions with a crash, and Joe sprawled in the debris. His grin turned into hysterical laughter as he held up a finger oozing blood.

He went suddenly quiet as the front door bell rang again.

"Quick!" Peter hissed. He pulled out his handkerchief, slapped it round Joe's bleeding finger, then half-pulled, half-pushed Joe, still in costume, back into the cupboard. He slammed the door. A muffled "Hoy!" from inside was followed by obedient silence. Peter retrieved the hall table and the telephone, trying not to notice the scrape marks on the wallpaper. He went to the front door again, opened it a few inches, peered through the crack.

It was, as he suspected, Mrs Spinks, his nosy next-door neighbour.

"Are you all right, dear? I thought I heard a crash?"

She was old and wrinkled, no taller than Peter. She stood on tiptoe trying to see over him into the hall. Peter weaved up and down, blocking her view.

"I didn't hear anything," he said. He stood his ground as she tried to inch forward into the house.

"Why did you have the curtain across? I looked through the letterbox to see what the noise was and couldn't see anything."

"It's cold. I'm keeping the heat in."

Mrs Spinks pressed forward again, but Peter resisted.

"Who else is there?"

"No one."

"I thought I saw Joe come?"

"He went."

"Your uncle said I could keep an eye on you when he's at work."

A likely story, thought Peter. *I bet you suggested it.*

16

"I want to see what the crash was."

"Nothing, honest."

"Well I'll come in anyway because I want to borrow some eggs."

"We haven't got any."

She squinted at him suspiciously.

"Are you sure?"

"Yes. We had the last ones for breakfast. I remember my uncle saying, 'That's all the eggs gone, I must get some more'."

Peter couldn't imagine his uncle saying any such thing in a million years.

"I need some flour as well."

"We haven't got any of that, either. I remember my uncle saying, 'Oh! And I must get some flour'."

"You might have a little bit left."

"No. I—" Peter improvised – "I saw him screw up the bag as he said it."

Mrs Spinks moved her foot into the space between the door and the frame as Peter tried to close the gap.

"Sugar, then. You must have some sugar?"

"No."

"Course you've got some sugar," said Mrs Spinks, getting annoyed. "Everyone's got sugar."

"Why haven't you got any, then?" said Peter, and immediately went red, realising he'd gone too far.

"You cheeky little so-and-so! How dare you!"

There followed a brief struggle. Peter had his foot jammed against the inside of the door, but it wasn't much good for very long. Mrs Spinks was short, but she was also powerful. She was adept at barging her way on to buses, and driving herself like a wedge through solid hordes at jumble sales. With a big shove she forced him back and made her way into the hall. She looked round suspiciously.

"I know you! You're up to something! And your uncle

17

said I can come in *any time* if I think there's something
Going On. I've still got the key your mother gave me, so
don't think you can shut me out."

"There's nothing going on!"

"There is!" She started walking along to the kitchen. "I'm
going to find your eggs, and your flour *and* your sugar! And
if I find you're lying about *them*, I'll know you're lying
about the crash!"

Peter paled. At least Joe was having the sense to keep
quiet, although he had heard a thump just as Mrs Spinks was
pushing past him. Now the old loony was going to nose in
the kitchen and find out he was making it all up. He
followed, keeping close.

Mrs Spinks opened the fridge. She was slightly taken
aback.

"Mmmm! No eggs."

"I told you!" said Peter. It was an unexpected stroke of
luck. He took courage from it. "I told you we didn't have
any. You didn't believe me!"

She closed the fridge and opened the cupboard. Her quick
little hands reached up, moving things. In a few seconds she
calmed down, her face changing from fury to
embarrassment.

"Oh!" she said, looking uncomfortable. "No flour, and –
goodness! – no sugar!"

Peter, amazed at his good fortune, celebrated with a few
mental handstands. He looked her straight in the eye.

"I'll have to tell my uncle about this."

"That's not necessary," said Mrs Spinks, hastily closing
the cupboard. She tried to move back towards the hall.

"It's bad manners not to believe people," added Peter,
blocking her exit route.

"I didn't say I didn't *believe* you . . ."

"And it's bad manners to push into somebody's house
without being invited. I'm going to tell my uncle."

Mrs Spinks finally escaped past him by going the other way round the kitchen table. She headed for the front door, then turned suddenly, digging into her purse.

"I don't think you need to mention this to your uncle, dear." She produced a pound coin and pressed it into his hand. "Do you?"

"No, perhaps not." He thought for a moment, looking down at the coin. He blinked once and added, "Joe's coming back soon . . ."

Mad as she was, Mrs Spinks knew blackmail when she heard it. She pressed another pound into the outstretched palm.

"There, now! Not a word!"

"No. Thank you, Mrs Spinks."

Peter saw her out, closed the front door and drew the curtain across. He opened the door under the stairs and bent down to give Joe his pound and the good news.

Joe was sprawled on the floor of the cupboard, still wrapped in his uncle's raincoat, but minus the hat. On his lap were a packet of sugar, a bag of flour and four loose eggs. One of the eggs had broken. It was dripping in disgusting blobs from the raincoat on to the linoleum.

"I only just got back in time!" Joe grinned.

CHAPTER TWO

In the Attic

Peter and Joe spent the next five minutes scrubbing the egg off the raincoat. Peter suddenly felt happier than he'd been for a long time. It was difficult to feel bad when Joe was around. His infectious grin and strong sense of anarchy helped a lot.

"Let's finish looking under the stairs," he said.

They stacked its contents in the hall, examining each article as they took it out.

"If he's hidden the parcel in here, we'll find it all right. No problem."

They went through the rest of the cupboard. Along with the paints there were tools, wellington boots, a vacuum cleaner, brooms and other cleaning equipment, a bag of old rags for dusters, a few pictures in broken frames and several boxes of screws and nails.

"Does your uncle do a lot of decorating, or something?" said Joe. His muffled voice came from near the floor in the deepest part of the cupboard.

"He never does anything except moan and look at himself in the mirror. Most of that old stuff belonged to Mum."

"Oh – yeah – of course."

Peter suppressed a sigh. Any mention of his mother still brought a lump to his throat. He swallowed it away as Joe emerged, dusty and creased.

"No birthday present in there."

It only confirmed Peter's already fading hopes. He couldn't imagine his uncle going to that much trouble for his birthday. His uncle didn't even know what "fun" meant.

Even if he *had* put himself out to buy a present, he certainly wouldn't put himself out to hide it deep in a cupboard.

"Come on, then," he said, his enthusiasm rapidly waning. "Let's try the bedrooms."

They put everything back roughly how they'd found it, and went upstairs. Only two bedrooms had cupboards, and Peter already knew what was in his own. The wardrobe in his uncle's room was full of new suits, new shoes, new ties, new shirts, new jumpers and new travelling cases.

They went back downstairs. The cupboard in the dining-room was full of glass and china, and the sitting-room cupboard was empty. As they walked out Peter glanced back at the picture of his mother on the mantelpiece, wishing he could make her come alive.

"Let's try the attic!" Joe suggested.

"All right." Peter certainly couldn't imagine his uncle bothering with the attic. Not in a million years. But it sounded like fun, anyway.

They went upstairs again, fetched the long pole from behind the spare room door, hooked it into the trap-door ring, and pulled. As it opened, cold air cascaded on to them like a waterfall. They unfolded the aluminium ladder and Joe followed Peter up the steps.

It was dark and gloomy. Peter had never been in the attic before. He'd watched his mother open it a few times. She'd let him climb to the top of the steps, but never right inside in case he went through the ceiling. He switched on the light, a dim, bare bulb that left most of the corners in shadow. He went back down to fetch a torch. When he returned, Joe was already kneeling on two of the joists under the eaves, groping round behind the chimney stack.

"Make sure you keep your feet on the beams," Joe warned, pulling at an unseen object. "I nearly put mine through the ceiling just now."

"Have you found something?"

"I think so."

"What is it?"

"It might be a cardboard box. It's hidden behind this thing and I can't see it properly."

"What's in it?"

"Don't know." He took the torch from Peter. "It's tied up with string. Do you think your mother put it here?"

"Don't know."

Peter knelt alongside as best he could, balancing on the joists.

"Let's get it out."

Joe stretched forward and pulled it up. It was heavy and dark with dust. Joe blew some of the dust towards Peter, and Peter retaliated by blowing some back. In the frantic dust-blowing battle that followed, all the dirt was transferred from the top of the box on to their faces, their necks, their hands, and their clothes.

"You look like a coal miner."

"You look like a chimney sweep."

They improved the game by scrambling from beam to beam, pursuing each other round the loft. They stopped for a rest, squatting one each side of another filthy surface. Joe's murky features split open into a wide grin as he shouted, "One, two, three, *blow*!" They both blew together, showering each other's faces with grime, each trying to out-blow the other.

"It's the opposite of vacuum-cleaning," announced Joe, snatching another breath. "Blow-cleaning!"

By the time they had blow-cleaned the water tank cover, the chimney ledge and most of the cross-beams, the air was thick with acrid particles that made them cough and splutter.

"It tastes horrible," said Peter, croaking.

Joe was licking his lips. "I quite like it, really."

"Well," said Peter at last, going back to the box, "this can't be my birthday present. This has been here for years."

"You look as if you've been here for years yourself. You're filthy."

"So are you. Perhaps we'd better have a wash before we open it."

They climbed down the ladder and cleaned up by transferring most of the dirt from themselves to the bathroom towel. Peter retrieved his handkerchief from Joe's finger, then they went downstairs to have a drink. Joe saw the time on the kitchen clock and shrieked.

"Oh no! I'm supposed to be helping in the shop in five minutes! Better go!"

"When you come back," Peter said, "we'll open the box."

Joe set off, whistling as he jogged. He glanced both ways and crossed the road towards a light green sports car that was parked further along on the other side. The top was open, and a man was sitting in the car, reading a newspaper. He looked up as Joe approached.

"Peter?" the man said, as Joe drew level.

Joe stopped, his whistling stopped, and his eyes stopped on the man.

"Don't look so worried," said the man. His voice was soft with a strange accent that Joe couldn't place. "I'm not going to offer you sweets or ask you to get in the car."

Joe stared, all the more suspicious.

"I'd call the police if you did," he said, "and tell them your number plate."

"I bet you don't know what it is."

"WOW 149," said Joe promptly.

The man seemed surprised.

"I see neighbourhood watch is working in this area, then," he commented. He smiled a weak smile and continued. "You're Peter, aren't you? I was told you lived in this road, but I can't read me own writing. I wasn't sure if it was number thirty-eight or twenty-eight?"

Joe glanced across at the piece of paper lying on the seat next to the man, where "28" was written in large, clear letters. His internal smoke alarm started clamouring.

He feigned ignorance.

"Peter who?"

"You came out of number twenty-eight. Aren't you Peter Briscoe?"

Joe pretended to think for a moment.

"Never heard of him," he muttered, and ran on before the man could ask him anything else.

Further down the road, Joe hid behind another car and looked back. The man had climbed out and was crossing the road to Peter's house.

The usual air of gloom settled over Peter almost as soon as Joe had gone. There was no birthday present. He'd found the brown paper wrapping behind the waste bin, and a brand new shaver in its box in the downstairs toilet. It wouldn't surprise him if his uncle didn't even know when his birthday was. Only a few days away now. Would he have to ask for a birthday present, the same way he had to ask for his pocket money every week? He went to the calendar and drew a big black ring round October 25th and wrote "Peter's Birthday."

Presently he heard the sound of a car door slamming not far away. He went to the front window. The light green sports car was back, and the man had climbed out. He was crossing the road towards the house.

He didn't like the look of the man at all. Peter dashed across the hall and up the stairs, waited at the top, panting.

The front doorbell rang.

Peter froze. The seconds passed and the doorbell rang again. More seconds, then the knocker. Peter breathed out slowly, crept to his uncle's bedroom window, and peered through the net curtains. He couldn't see the porch from there, but he could see the path and the gate. The doorbell rang once more, then the man appeared out on the path, turning to look up at the windows. He was wearing sporty clothes to go with his sporty car. Peter thought he couldn't have behaved much more suspiciously if he'd tried. As soon as the man reached the gate, nosy Mrs Spinks appeared.

Peter watched, but couldn't hear the conversation. He thought of opening the window, but it would make a noise and attract their attention. The man was pointing up at the house, then turning and pointing the way Joe had gone. Mrs Spinks seemed to have lots to say, as usual. Peter heard her shrill voice piping up, but couldn't distinguish the words. She went back into her house and emerged with a key. She held it up in the air – the spare key to Peter's house that she'd been given for emergencies. What was the old crackpot doing?

Peter knew what *he* was doing. He climbed the steps into the attic, pulled up the ladder, and lifted the trap-door shut. He lay on the planks, breathing hard and listening. There were muffled voices, then the sound of a key turning. The front door opened and the voices became more distinct.

"Now you stay there," Mrs Spinks commanded, "and I'll see if he's out the back. He might be lying *injured* somewhere. He might not be able to *move*."

She entered the house, calling. He heard her come upstairs, then go back down and out again. The front door slammed, and Peter heard little footsteps on the path outside. At least she hadn't let the man in the house.

It was funny how he could hear their voices better from the attic than when he'd been in the bedroom.

"No sign of him." Mrs Spinks' voice was shrill. "He must have gone over the back wall, naughty boy. Mrs Patterson over there won't like that."

"His mother died recently, didn't she?" said the man. His voice was smooth and slightly accented, northern.

"Six weeks ago. All of a sudden, too. Taken ill, and a

week later she was gone, just like that. Poor Peter. He never had a father, poor lad. It was lucky his uncle lived local. Of course, he gave up his rented flat and came to live here with Peter – to look after him. He's a businessman, you know, Mr Briscoe is. Very respectable-looking. P'rhaps I shouldn't be telling you all this, I don't know who you are. Who are you?"

"I'm an old friend of Deirdre Briscoe. I heard she had died, and . . ."

"Deirdre *Briscoe*? You must have known her before she was married, then. Mrs Turner she was, to us. Not that I ever saw *Mr* Turner. Dunno what happened to *him*."

"I, er – I used to know Miss Briscoe when she lived in Chichester."

"Oh. Is that where she came from? I always thought she was local."

"Well, thanks for all your help."

"You might catch Peter's uncle – Mr Briscoe – just after one o'clock," said Mrs Spinks. "He sometimes comes home for lunch. You'll catch Peter, then, as well."

"Thank you."

There were footsteps in the road, then the sound of a car door slamming – and silence.

Peter lay in the dusty loft a little while longer. When he came down, the sports car was still there and the man was still watching the house.

CHAPTER THREE

Birthday Past

Peter had a bath, put on clean clothes, rinsed the dirty towel in the bath water and hung it up to dry on the rail.

When another twenty minutes had passed and Joe still hadn't come back, Peter rang his house. Joe's mother answered.

"Is Joe there, please?"

"Yes, he is," came the calm, long-suffering female voice. "Is that Peter?"

"Yes."

"Well, Peter, I don't know what you two get up to when he comes round your house, but he came home *filthy*!"

Peter went into defence mode.

"We didn't do anything."

"Well, if you didn't do anything, you must have discovered the world's first magnetic dirt," retorted Joe's mother. "I couldn't let him go to the shop like that. He can come over again when he's cleaned himself properly and done some other jobs to make up for it."

Peter sighed into the telephone.

"Thank you. Bye."

He was tempted to look in the box without Joe, but he'd promised to wait until they could do it together.

Two hours later, the front doorbell rang again. He looked through the net curtain in the hall. Joe was there, but the man was still sitting in the green sports car, watching Joe's every move. Peter stooped down and whispered through the letterbox.

"Ring the doorbell again, and wait a bit. Then look as if

you're going away. Then sneak round the back."

Joe seemed to recognise the urgency in Peter's voice.

"What's up?" he whispered.

"That green sports car across the road – he's watching the house – don't look now, stupid!"

"Sorry."

"Just go away. Pretend you couldn't get an answer. Then sneak round the side without him seeing you."

Joe turned obediently and walked away. Ten minutes later Peter greeted him at the back door.

"Well done! Did you have any trouble?"

"Had to climb over six fences," Joe said proudly. "What's all the secrecy?"

Peter told him about the sports car and the man. Joe told Peter how the man had questioned him, and about the piece of paper lying on the seat next to him.

"He thought I was you," Joe finished. "That proves he's never seen you, because we're nothing like each other. I'm tall, fair and good-looking, and you're short, dark and ugly."

Peter retorted with a withering stare.

"What do you think he wants?" Joe added.

"How should I know? I didn't like the look of him from the start. He looks sneaky. He shouldn't sit watching other people's houses, for one thing."

"They do in spy films."

"I suppose I'll have to tell the carbuncle when he gets home."

Joe was anxious to get on.

"I know," he said, "let's put the bolt across the door so old Mrs Spinks can't get in again. Then we can go and look in that box."

As Joe was shooting the bolt, a flicker of anxiety passed across Peter's face.

"What's the matter?" said Joe.

"I've got a funny feeling about that box. I don't think we

28

should open it."

"What? Come on, it'll be really spooky. I bet we find a skull in it, or a skeleton hand, or—"

"Shut up, Joe."

They were interrupted by the sound of the sports car starting up, closely followed by a roar as it sped off down the road.

"Oh, good," said Peter, cheering up again. "At least *he's* gone."

They climbed into the attic. Balancing on the beams, they carefully untied the string round the box and opened the flaps.

"It's been here a long time," said Joe. "Look! Mice have been nibbling it."

It was true. One of the lower corners had been eaten away, leaving a gaping hole.

They took it in turns to take things out. Peter went first.

"What is it?"

"A tin of money," Peter said, rattling it.

"Great! Let's have a look!"

Peter opened the lid. Inside were dozens of huge copper pennies, some still shiny from the 1960s, some dull with Kings' heads, and a few worn smooth with Queen Victoria's outline.

"It's old money."

"Twelve of those big pennies made a shilling," said Joe.

"Twenty shillings made a pound," said Peter, not to be outdone. "And look at this one!" He held up a small golden twelve-sided coin, thick and heavy.

"That's a threepenny bit," said Joe.

They spent five minutes feeling what it was like to have the heavy old money in their hands and their pockets. Then Joe made a stack of twelve pennies and said, "Bet you can't do this!" He rose unsteadily to his feet, balancing on the joists. He raised his right hand near his ear until his elbow stuck out level at the front, then balanced the stack of pennies on the end.

"Ready?" His hand whirred forward as he tried to catch the pennies in mid-air.

Peter ducked as the big coins shot off Joe's elbow like bullets, scattering in all directions, bouncing off beams and disappearing into the half gloom.

"You idiot!"

They spent the next ten minutes looking for the pennies.

"If you find one dated 1933 it's worth thousands," came Joe's voice, muffled by loft insulation.

They spent another ten minutes checking the dates of all the pennies in the tin.

"Just about every date since 1892, but no 1933," said Peter. "Just our luck."

Then it was Joe's turn to take something from the cardboard box. He reached inside.

"What've you got?"

"An album of picture cards," said Joe in disgust. "Wild flowers. What's yours?"

Peter dipped in.

"A skipping rope."

"Fancy keeping a skipping rope!"

"What's next?"

"A photograph album."

Peter took it and flicked through the pages.

"No one in it I've ever seen before, except my mum. Not even carbuncle Len." He placed it carefully to one side, reached into the box again and said, "Three records. All Elvis Presley." Joe sang a snatch from each title, then Peter said, "Your turn."

"Yuk of yuks!" exclaimed Joe. "A Valentine card!"

"Don't look in it," said Peter anxiously, but he was too late.

"It doesn't say anything much," said Joe, reading it. "Just

a sloppy poem."

Suddenly, Peter began to feel uneasy again. He retrieved the photograph album and stared at the pictures of his mother, much younger. He felt the beginnings of tears jerking behind his eyes and closed the album before they could get any worse. The skipping rope was probably his mother's as well. She'd probably kept it since she was a girl. The more he looked at the objects in the box, the more he began to not like what they were doing.

"I don't think we should look at some of these things," he said, his voice shaky. "They're private."

Joe threw the Valentine card on the growing pile.

"Sorry."

Peter nervously pulled out a small book, feeling less and less inclined to look at anything at all. He wanted to put everything back in the box and go down.

"*You've found a diary!*" he heard Joe saying. "Let's have a look!"

Peter looked down and saw the diary in his hand. He flipped it open, then snapped it shut again.

"We'd better not look at anything else," he said, his voice breaking. He felt his skin beginning to prickle with goose bumps.

"Why not?"

"I just – well, I just don't think we should."

"*But why?* It can't do any harm."

Peter was staring at the diary.

"*It's got my mum's handwriting on the front*, that's why. It's private. That's probably why she hid it up here."

"Like the skipping rope," mocked Joe. "I suppose *that's* private."

"You know what I mean."

"No, I don't. Anyway, it might say something about your dad."

Despite the uneasy feeling in his stomach, Peter suddenly

felt interested again. Interested, but still frightened. Ever since his mother had died all those weeks ago, he had become more and more curious about his father. His mother had never spoken of him, other than to say he was dead. If Peter ever asked any questions she had always looked hurt and said his father wasn't worth talking about.

He looked at Joe. Joe's face was animated and eager, thirsting for excitement. Joe was right. It might say something about his father.

"Yes, it might," he said.

"What year's the diary?" said Joe.

Peter glanced at the cover. His mouth dropped open as he looked across at his friend in the dim light.

"*It's the year I was born.*"

With shaking fingers, Peter opened the diary and started turning the pages. It had his mother's single name at the front, "Deirdre Briscoe". All the January pages were blank, so he carried on, looking for the first entry. He found it on February the twentieth. It said one word: "Pregnant".

"That's when she first knew," said Joe, grinning. "I bet she didn't know then what a dope you'd turn out to be."

A short friendly wrestle followed, which helped Peter feel better again, then they went back to the diary.

But Peter's unease rapidly returned. He didn't know whether it was just natural shyness, or reaction to Joe's irreverence, or a real sense of foreboding. His hands shook again as he held the diary, turning more pages.

"March the twenty-second: 'Sick of being sick.' What does that mean?"

"What it says, of course. What do you think it means? It means she spewed up like a sewage pipe every morning, and she was sick of it."

"Oh." Peter thumbed forward, feeling that his mother being sick was all his fault. "June the fourteenth: 'Can't eat enough bananas.' June the twentieth: 'Bananas out.

32

Custard in'." He turned to Joe. "I don't understand half of it."

"Let me read some," said Joe, still grinning. He made a grab for the diary, but Peter reacted and swung it out of his reach.

"No, it's still my turn. Anyway, it's my mum's *private* diary, so I should read it, not you."

"What does it say about when you were born?"

"I haven't got to October yet. I'm still on July. July the thirtieth: 'Hot. Went to the Witterings for the day. Too fat to get into swimming costume. Frank swam and windsurfed'."

"Was Frank your father?"

Peter blushed hot, feeling insecure.

"I don't know. My mum never even told me his name. She said he wasn't worth knowing."

"Well, you *should* know. He might be alive, and your mother didn't tell you. And *he* might not know your mother died."

Peter shrugged. He didn't risk saying anything in case his voice cracked up again and Joe noticed. He sneaked a few quiet deep breaths, turning the pages nearer and nearer to the day he was born.

"August the eleventh: 'Baby kicked me while I was eating ice cream. Think he wanted some. Only kicks when it's strawberry'."

"Does it mention Frank again?"

Peter was turning the pages faster, scanning down each one, his hands trembling more and more.

"I don't think so."

"What does it say on your birthday, then?"

Peter found it. Smiled.

"Here I am," he said. "October the twenty-fifth: 'A wonderful, lovely, marvellous baby boy. Seven pounds, one ounce. PETER'." Then Peter's brief smile faded.

"'*Something wrong, they can't say what, yet*'." He turned to Joe. "I didn't know I was ill when I was born."

He turned the page to the following day and read the words. Prickles rose on the back of his head, travelling across his shoulders and down his back. He was suddenly as cold as an iceberg. The diary fell from his hands.

"What's the matter?" said Joe, concerned. "You look ill. Are you okay?"

Peter stared at him, unable to speak, his neck and jaw muscles paralysed and his eyes filling with tears. Joe, alarmed, picked up the diary from where it had fallen and frantically turned the pages to October the twenty-fifth, Peter's birthday. As he turned over to the next day, he read the same words that Peter had found.

"'October the twenty-sixth: *Today my poor baby Peter died*'."

CHAPTER FOUR

Runaway Joe

Joe stared at the words, trying to make them mean something else, something less horrible. But nothing came.

Today my poor baby Peter died.

They meant what they said. He looked across at Peter, who had gone deathly quiet and was looking really odd. Joe thumbed the pages backwards to see if it really was Peter's mother's diary.

"Perhaps it's not hers," he said in a weak voice, hoping.

Peter looked up with the moisture in his eyes flashing yellow in the torchlight.

"Of course it's hers," he said. His throat felt as if he'd swallowed a sandpaper block. "I told you. It's her handwriting."

"It could be someone who wrote like she did."

"It's got her *name* in it."

There was a pause, then Joe said, "It could be someone with the *same name*, who wrote like your mum. And your mum found it at a jumble sale and was *amazed* because . . ." His voice had quickened, but now it trailed off.

" . . .because she had a son called *Peter*," said Peter with heavy sarcasm, finishing the thought for him, "who was born on the *same day. Brilliant*! I can just believe it!"

Joe fiddled with the diary for a few seconds, turning the pages, trying hard to think of other possibilities.

"She hasn't written anything after that," he said. "The rest of it's empty."

"I don't suppose she had anything else to write about," said Peter, miserably. "I was *dead*!"

Joe looked at him closely.

"You don't *look* very dead," he said, trying hard to make light of it. "I know you behave like you're *mentally* dead sometimes, but you seem to be moving okay at the moment."

"*It's not a joke!*" said Peter, fiercely. "*Don't you understand?*" He snarled the words, glaring at his friend while the knife that was cutting his insides started writhing in the wound.

Undaunted, Joe growled back at him.

"Of course it's a joke! What are you getting all upset about, stupid? *You can't be dead, can you?* You're *here.*" Joe's anarchic humour rose to new heights of sarcasm. "I'll get a mirror if you like and you can poke your tongue out at your own dead body. Look! Me dead. Me laughing." Joe leaned across and made silly grinning faces.

Peter looked away. He was still feeling miserable, but a smile – or perhaps it was a sob – erupted inside him. Whatever it was, he didn't like it, and tried to suppress it.

"Well," said Joe, noticing, "that's the first time I've ever seen a corpse trying not to laugh."

Peter stared gloomily into the dark corners of the attic, soaking himself in misery. Under the black eaves, bright pinpricks of light were burning his eyes. Suddenly, there was a tangible silence, as if someone had switched off the world. Fragments of forgotten dreams drifted through his mind. He'd never heard the voice in his head in the daytime before, but he heard it now, echoing like the ghostly beat of a steam train winding through a mountain valley. The drumming hurt his ears, and for once he could almost grasp the voice, almost hear what it was saying. "*Peter! Peter!*" He found himself wondering if darkness and silence and voices and madness were all the same thing.

"*Peter! Peter!*" It was Joe shaking him, not the voice. Not the voice calling him "Peter". Joe.

"God, I thought you'd gone into a trance." Joe was saying it, pale as a ghost. "You had me worried. You went right off."

Peter blinked at Joe slowly as his head swam back to reality and the beating in his head faded to nothing.

"It doesn't make *sense*," he said quietly, at last. "The diary says I died, but I'm here. It's *stupid*."

"That's what I told you three minutes ago," said Joe, relieved to hear Peter talking normally again. "Anyway, I've just thought of something else."

"What? Not something ridiculous?"

"Would I ever?" said Joe innocently. He said it as if saying ridiculous things was something he never did in his whole life. "Didn't you say your father died before you were born?"

"So Mum said."

"And you don't know his name?"

"No."

"Your mum didn't tell you?"

"No. She always said he died before I was born, that's all. She never wanted to talk about him."

"Well, s'pose he died just *after* you were born – the very next day? If his name was Peter, the diary might mean it was *him* who died."

Peter looked up in brief hope, then sagged again, unconvinced.

"Poor *baby* Peter?" he reminded him.

"Well," said Joe, thinking, then coming up with an answer. "People used to call each other 'baby' in those days, didn't they? What about songs like *Maybe Baby* that my mum's always singing, or *Baby, Baby, Can't You Hear My Heart Beat*? and things like that?"

Seeing that Peter was unimpressed, Joe gave a brief rendition of each song to jog his memory. He balanced on the beams and swung from side to side until he slipped and almost put his foot through the ceiling again.

"Baby, baby, can't you hear my heart – *whoops*!"

"*Stop being stupid*!" Peter shouted. He felt annoyed, but he wasn't really annoyed with Joe. He knew Joe was only trying to cheer him up, trying to find a way of taking his mind off the horrible, world-changing entry in the diary. That's what Joe was like. Peter only felt cross with himself now, and cross with his mother for dying and leaving him alone in the world. He quickly rubbed a sleeve across his eyes.

"It doesn't make sense, does it?" he said at last, more or less calmly. At least with Joe around he couldn't dwell on anything morbid for long.

"No, it doesn't," said Joe.

Peter looked at his watch.

"Anyway, Fish-face will be home for lunch soon. We'd better go down. We can leave everything out and come back afterwards."

They closed the trap-door and Joe went home.

Gloom settled on Peter again as soon as his uncle was due. He went into the kitchen and made himself a pile of cheese and golden syrup sandwiches, hoping he could eat them before his uncle came home. As the pile of sandwiches diminished, he wondered if the rest of his life would be like this – not only living with a man who made his flesh creep – but now, forever wondering about the frightening entry in his mother's diary.

The diary made him think of his mother's letter.

His fingers wandered to his shirt, moving up and down, feeling the envelope. Now that he'd found the diary, the letter made more sense . . .

He glanced at the clock. It was already past the time when his uncle usually came home for lunch. Perhaps he was eating out.

Peter reached inside his collar and pulled out the stiff brown envelope. He lifted the flap, slid out the precious sheet of paper, and read it for the forty-second time:

My Darling Peter,

When you read this, you'll know that I am gone. I didn't expect to be leaving you, and I hoped that there would never be any reason for you to be given this letter. But here it is. I wrote it just in case. I've left it with the will and told the solicitor to give it to you privately to make sure you can keep it to yourself if you want to.

It breaks my heart to tell you that I've left you with a secret. Perhaps you'll find it one day. If you do, I hope you can work out what it means, because I could never bring myself to tell you, or anyone, then or now.

Be brave and grow honest and strong and find it in your heart to forgive me, darling.

I love you.

Mum.

Peter folded the letter carefully, replaced it inside the envelope, and dropped the packet inside his shirt. He still didn't understand the letter, but he thought he understood it better. Now he felt sure that the diary had something to do with it.

His uncle didn't come home at lunch-time. It sometimes happened that way, and every time it did Peter felt relieved. He felt relieved now. Joe returned soon after two o'clock, and they went straight back into the attic.

"Did you ask your uncle anything?" said Joe. They were sitting cross-legged with the dusty box between them.

"He didn't come home."

"Oh."

"Where's the diary?"

"Under your knee. What've you thought of now?"

"Well," Joe began, "if your father died *before* you were born, it'll be mentioned in the diary, won't it?"

39

"I suppose so."

Joe grinned.

"So we'll have to read it all."

Peter groaned.

"I suppose so."

Joe read in silence for a while, then laughed.

"June the fourteenth. 'Gone off cheese, but can't stop eating peanuts. Perhaps I'm having a monkey'." He looked up at Peter. "She was right."

Peter smiled more out of friendship than seeing anything funny as Joe handed him the book. By the time Peter had reached the last fateful entry they had found no reference to his father's death.

"If he *had* died before I was born, you'd think she'd *mention* it," said Peter.

"I don't think your father's dead," said Joe, simply.

Peter considered.

"Well, there's *something* wrong. There's something about it that Mum never told me. She *could* have, but she didn't *want* to."

"There's another funny thing as well," said Joe.

"What?"

"Your mother's maiden name is in the diary, right?"

"Yes."

"Deirdre *Briscoe*, right?"

"Yes."

"So why are you called Peter Briscoe, then, when your mother was Mrs Turner? Why aren't you Peter *Turner*?"

"I dunno – I thought . . . well, I'd never thought much about it. There's plenty of other kids with different names from their mums and dads."

Joe shrugged.

"I wonder if there's anything else in the box that might give us a clue?"

Peter thought of his mother's letter again and was suddenly

interested.

"There might be." He picked up the box and scooped its remaining contents on to the few planks that surrounded the attic trap-door. He waved away the clouds of dust and smoothed the newspaper that lined the bottom of the box, its corner chewed away by the long-ago mouse. They went through the other papers one by one, putting them back in the box afterwards.

"What's this?" said Peter. He held up a stiffish sheet of paper. "'This is to certify that Miss Deirdre Ann Briscoe has passed the St John's Ambulance course in First Aid.'"

"There! That shows your mother was a Miss."

"What do you mean?"

"When she had you, she wasn't married. If she was *Miss* Briscoe, and you're Peter *Briscoe* . . ." Joe left the sentence unfinished. He had already pulled out another sheet and was reading it. "Hey! Look at this!"

"What is it?"

Peter looked. It was his mother's birth certificate. He took it and read aloud.

"'*Date of birth, 10th February; Names, Deirdre Ann; Father, Peter Henry Briscoe; Occupation, labourer. Mother, Caroline Primrose Briscoe; Occupation, housewife.*'" Peter looked up. "That's funny, though."

"What?"

"Keeping her birth certificate in this dusty old box in the attic. Wouldn't she need it handy for passports and things?"

"Yes, funny, that," agreed Joe. "Anyway – her father was called Peter. So she must have named you after him."

Peter felt the gloom creeping up on him again. "I don't see how that helps," he said, "if I'm dead."

"Where's *your* birth certificate?" said Joe. "That might tell us something. It's probably here somewhere." He scrambled through the dwindling pile, looking for another piece of paper folded in three.

Peter felt his frustration rising to the surface.

"Well, why did she call herself Mrs *Turner*, then? It doesn't make sense. None of it makes sense."

"Perhaps she just called herself Mrs Turner because it was easier. Some single mothers call themselves Ms or Miss, but your mum preferred to be Mrs."

Peter suddenly felt frightened again. He'd had more unpleasant shocks in the last few hours than in the whole of his life before, except for when his mother had died. It left him feeling unsettled and hurt. He had always believed that his father was dead. Now, he had the strangely disturbing thought that his father might be alive somewhere . . .

He came out of his reverie and looked across at Joe. To his amazement he found his friend's perennial grin disappearing and his face turning chalky white. Joe had found another certificate and was staring at it, and his sudden shocked glance at Peter was ringing alarm bells.

"Nothing interesting," Joe said, but he said it too hastily. He pushed whatever-it-was into the box, but Peter had seen the look and the too-hasty movement.

"What was that?" said Peter. His eyes swivelled to the box where Joe had pushed the paper in. The certificate was still sticking out at one corner. He reached over for it, but Joe's hand slammed down on his.

"No!" he said. He stared straight into Peter's eyes.

"I want to look at it! What is it?"

"*Don't*!" shouted Joe. "*Get off*!"

Peter made a grab with his other hand but Joe pinned it down. Peter brought his legs up and tried to get his feet into Joe's chest to lever him off, but Joe's legs unfolded and pushed them away. They wrestled on the narrow planks, sometimes going dangerously close to the open hatch, sometimes rolling towards the gaps in the beams that surrounded the little platform. Peter made another grab for the paper, but Joe bulldozed him away, feet scrabbling on the beams. Then Joe got his hand to the box and scattered the contents in all directions.

"*It's my mum's paper and I want to see it*!" screamed Peter.

He saw where the paper had landed and made another lunge for it. For a moment he held it in his hand, but Joe fell on top of his arm and started twisting the paper away.

"Don't! You'll tear it!"

"Good! You mustn't look at it!"

With a mighty heave, Joe pulled at the paper. It was thick and didn't tear, and came away clean from Peter's hand. But even as Joe held it up triumphantly and tried to clamber off his friend, Peter stretched up and grabbed it back with his other hand. He was nearest the hatchway. His mind calculated quickly, and he threw it into the gaping hole.

Joe saw what he had done and rolled him over, trying to get to the ladder first himself. They fought and struggled, the ladder swaying from side to side as they both pushed and pulled and grappled and tried to get the advantage of the other.

Finally, Peter plunged down the steps, Joe above him treading on his hands – anything to stop him getting to the paper. Even as Peter stooped to pick it up, Joe came rolling down on top of him like a beer barrel and flattened him out.

Peter was winded. Joe made a quick movement and grabbed the paper. He tumbled down the stairs and out through the front door, slamming it behind him.

By the time Peter had regained his breath, Joe was gone.

CHAPTER FIVE

The Man in the Green Sports Car

Peter stood on the half-landing staring at the slammed front door. Joe's sudden departure had not helped his feeling of gloom. It had left him feeling scared.

Joe had never run off like that – ever. Joe was a good friend. His best friend. Joe always stayed around till the bitter end, always. Why had he deserted him now, after all the disturbing discoveries . . .? Peter shook his head in disbelief. Without Joe, he didn't know what to do.

In a daze, he clumped slowly down the stairs, his legs shaking. For the first time he noticed his knuckles hurting where Joe had trodden on them – and his chest as well, where Joe's knee had rammed into it. He was conscious of breathing shallow and fast. His face was red hot, yet a cold feeling had settled over his shoulders.

He looked at his watch. Twenty past five. His uncle wouldn't be home for another forty minutes, at least.

Half in a dream, Peter mounted the steps into the attic once more. He found the diary again and went through its pages one by one, looking for some clue, just something that would make it *not* his mother's diary, or *not* his own birthday, or *not* his death the day after. But no matter how hard he looked, it *was* his mother's diary . . .

The chill in his shoulders had not disappeared, and it grew worse when he heard the familiar throaty sound of a sports car approaching. He slipped down from the attic, limped to the net curtains in his bedroom and peered out. His heart jumped when he saw that the light green sports car had drawn up by the kerb right outside the house. His uncle

Len's car was already in the driveway. His uncle was standing at the side of it, waiting for the man in the sports car – waiting for the very same man who had been watching the house – the same man who had asked Joe if he was Peter Briscoe.

Peter panicked. He tumbled back up the steps into the attic. He didn't dare leave anything lying about in case someone went up there. He couldn't imagine his uncle ever going up there, but some instinct told him that the box held the key to the secret – the secret his mother had mentioned in the letter. He had to conceal the box. There wasn't time to hide everything and to get down from the attic and close it before his uncle came in.

He did the next best thing. He pulled the ladder up and closed the trap-door from the inside, just as he had done earlier that morning. Seconds after it was shut he heard the sound of a key in the front door and his uncle's voice in the hall.

"Pete!"

Peter hated being called Pete. He lay on the few planks, breathing heavily. He kept his mouth wide open, gasping air in and out without making a noise.

"Pete!"

He felt the dry dust penetrating his lungs. He swallowed, but his mouth was dry and he wanted to cough.

"Pete! Are you in?"

Another voice came drifting up, the man's.

"Doesn't sound as if he is," it said.

Why was the man there? Why had his uncle brought him in?

"You'd better come inside."

"Thanks." The man's voice again.

"He'll be back soon. He usually gets back about now for his tea."

The front door closed. There were faint sounds of cups

45

rattling in the kitchen. Muffled voices. The way was as clear as it would ever be. Slowly and carefully, Peter felt for the torch and stood up. He gathered up the papers that had been scattered across the attic and replaced them in the dusty old cardboard box. As he replaced each one he looked at it again to see if he had missed anything important. There was nothing. At intervals he stopped and listened. He could still hear sounds from the kitchen and the murmur of voices.

At last the box was full. He closed the lid, tied up the string again and manoeuvred the box behind the chimney stack where Joe had found it. The sounds from the kitchen had faded. Suddenly a door opened and voices passed through the hall.

" . . .he's quiet, almost too quiet, but I'm trying to knock it out of him . . ."

"I'd love to meet him. I'm very interested in children . . ."

Another door closed and the voices were cut off abruptly.

Peter felt his heart thumping in his chest as he slowly opened the trap-door and listened. The voices were indistinct, coming from the sitting-room. He didn't want to risk using the noisy ladder, so he lowered himself over the edge of the hole. He clung on first with his stomach, then his elbows, and finally his hands. When he was at full stretch he dropped down with a little thud on to the carpet. He grabbed the hook and pushed up the trap-door until it clicked.

The sitting-room door creaked open.

"Is that you, Pete?" His uncle's voice.

Peter slipped into his bedroom and called from there.

"Ye-es!" He tried to sound normal, but his voice came out with a strange edge to it.

"You just come in?"

"Ye-es."

"I didn't see you come up the path."

"I came in the back."

46

"I've told you not to climb over those people's fences."

"Sorry."

"Will you come down? There's someone I want you to meet."

Peter went down and his uncle led him into the sitting-room. Peter trailed behind, his face pink from a hurried scrub, his hair hastily combed free of dust and cobwebs.

"Peter, I want you to meet Mr Woods."

The man from the light green sports car stood up. He didn't look as chubby close up. Around his moustache his face was creased with a false, over-friendly, salesman's sort of grin, a lot different from the grimace he'd had when he'd been watching the house.

Peter's dislike of him increased. He looked the sort of man who'd soon be asking stupid questions to "make conversation". He gripped Peter's hand and gave it a "manly" shake up and down, at the same time slapping Peter's shoulder with the other.

"Hello, Peter. Nice to make your acquaintance," said Mr Woods. "I like your T-shirt! Most amusing!"

The thin lips smiled and the eyes tried to twinkle, but Peter didn't trust them. He kept his face straight and mumbled a greeting.

"Mr Woods is here to discuss a business proposition," his uncle explained.

Peter remained silent, while his uncle strutted back and forth looking pleased with himself.

"Mr Woods has some interesting ideas that could make us all rich, Peter. Now – why don't you two have a little chat while I make some proper tea?"

With that, his uncle disappeared into the kitchen, leaving Peter and Mr Woods to square up to each other like David and Goliath.

Mr Woods cleared his throat.

"I bet you like football," he began in a friendly voice.

"You look the sort who likes football. Sturdy legs. Slim, fast frame."

"Well, I don't."

"Oh dear!" Mr Woods seemed taken aback. "How about cricket?"

"It's boring."

"Cricket? Never! Cricket's not boring – it can be very exciting . . ."

"No it can't."

Mr Woods' friendly voice withered slightly.

"I can see we're going to have to differ on that one. Cricket's a game you have to get used to. What about athletics, then?"

"I hate athletics," said Peter, lying.

"Oh, come, you must like *something*. What sports *do* you like?"

"None."

"I don't believe that. *All* boys like some sport or other. You must remember I was a boy myself once."

"Well, you're not a boy now," thought Peter.

There was an uncomfortable silence. Peter noticed that Mr Woods' eyes kept flitting round the room as he talked, taking everything in. His eyes had settled on the photograph of Peter's mother on the mantelpiece.

"Who's that nice looking lady?" he said.

Peter didn't feel like answering. Instead, he stared at Mr Woods' shoes, brown with buckles.

"Don't want to answer that one, eh? All right. You don't have to mind me. I'm just a nosy parker. I always had a great curiosity about things when I was little, and it's stayed with me ever since. I must have been a right pain to my parents." Mr Woods paused, then added suddenly, "And what about your father? Where does he work?"

Peter turned his gaze to look straight into the man's eyes, trying to read them. There was something more in the

48

question than just polite conversation. He was probing, pushing, trying to get information, and Peter didn't know why. He stayed on his guard.

"I haven't got a father," he said.

"Oh, I'm sorry. I didn't realise. Do you have a photograph of him?"

"No."

"That's a pity. Did they get lost?"

"Yes," Peter lied.

"Oh, well, another time," murmured Mr Woods. He seemed to have lost some of his forced friendliness. But then he took a deep breath and switched it all on again, the smile shining out like a string of fairground lights.

"What subjects do you like at school, then?"

"None."

"Don't like school, eh?"

"No."

The new-born smile on Mr Woods' face was already starting to fade.

"What *do* you like, then?" he challenged, trying to turn the tables. "You *must* like *some*thing."

Peter, undeterred, continued to meet Mr Woods' eyes without blinking.

"I like being alone," he said.

Mr Woods' smile disappeared completely and his pale blue eyes glinted like stainless steel, cold and sharp. The effect only lasted a split second, but Peter didn't miss it. The visitor's eyelids had flickered like a camera shutter before changing back to being friendly.

"Excuse me," Peter mumbled suddenly, and left the room.

He pretended to go upstairs, but crept back and watched Mr Woods through the crack near the hinges.

He saw Mr Woods pick up the photograph of his mother, turn it over to look at the back, replace it. He saw Mr Woods glance furtively towards the door, take something from his

49

pocket and hold it up. It might have been a camera, but Peter wasn't sure.

He walked back in, noisily blowing his nose. He saw Mr Woods hastily slip whatever-it-was back into his pocket.

"Ah, there you are!" Mr Woods said, sounding guilty.

Peter turned his handkerchief over to avoid the patch of blood from Joe's finger, when something extraordinary happened. Mr Woods' friendliness suddenly soared, with the cloying smile back at full strength.

"Here," he said, "don't use that filthy thing . . ."

"What?" Peter paused with his hanky in mid-air.

"That hanky. It's dirty. Give it here."

Mr Woods pulled a clean folded handkerchief from his own pocket and offered it, grabbing Peter's soiled one before Peter could think.

"That's better," said Mr Woods, handing over the new one. "You don't want to blow your nose with this dirty thing. You'll get all sorts of germs. I'll put it into the wash."

He hastily popped it into his pocket as Peter blew his nose. Then, before Peter had a chance to recover, his uncle came back into the room. He looked completely out of place carrying a tea tray and sandwiches and cakes.

"There!" he said. His voice was so bright it made Peter feel physically sick. "Let's have some tea."

Shortly after that, Mr Woods' mobile telephone rang in his pocket. He answered it curtly, then announced he'd have to leave right away.

"I left my car coat in the kitchen, I think," he added.

"Peter," said his uncle, "fetch Mr Woods' coat, will you?"

Peter walked slowly to the kitchen and fetched the coat, delaying a few seconds while he felt in the pockets. There was nothing there of interest. He handed the coat to his uncle who had come into the hall ahead of the visitor.

It seemed as if Mr Woods couldn't get out of the house fast enough after that. He gave a final sickening smile at Peter, shook hands with his uncle, and was gone. Uncle Len closed the front door and seconds later they heard the sports car roar into life and disappear into the distance.

Joe turned left out of Peter's house and ran and ran down the road, looking back to see if Peter was chasing him. He ran two blocks, then stopped in a gateway and checked again. There was no sign of Peter in pursuit. He stood regaining his breath for a few minutes, then slowly walked home. He went into the kitchen for a drink and some biscuits, then switched on the television. But he wasn't watching it. He couldn't take his mind off what he had found – the piece of paper tucked inside his shirt. After twenty minutes he switched off the TV and walked slowly back to Peter's house, thinking.

As he approached, he saw the light green sports car outside, empty. Peter's uncle's car was in the driveway. He wondered if Peter was all right.

He crept into the front garden and pushed his head into the large shrub that grew outside the window, then slowly raised himself up. The man and Peter's uncle were sitting in armchairs, Peter was sitting on a dining chair, and they were all having tea.

Joe slowly lowered himself again, then sidled out towards the sports car and looked inside. Its top was rolled down, and the doors weren't locked, so Joe sat in the driver's seat and pretended for a few seconds that he was driving it at a hundred and thirty miles an hour through the streets of Monte Carlo. When he returned to reality, he opened the glove compartment.

There on top was the same piece of paper he had seen on the seat that morning. He read it, all of it, this time:

Mrs Caroline Turner
28 Ford Avenue

51

(Miss Deirdre Briscoe??)

Mrs Turner, of course, was Peter's mother. But why had the man written *Miss Deirdre Briscoe* with question marks? And why Mrs *Caroline* Turner when she was known to everyone as Mrs *Deirdre* Turner? According to her birth certificate in the attic, Caroline wasn't one of her names at all.

Joe stared at the note for a few more moments, then put it on the seat beside him. His hand delved into the glove compartment again.

This time he found an A-Z map book of London. There was a rubber band keeping the page open, and a big circle in pencil round Peter's road. Further on in the map book was a torn out newspaper cutting. It said:

BRISCOE, Deirdre Ann. Died on 9th September after a short illness. Much loved by brother Len and son Peter (12). The funeral took place today (Thursday).

Joe wondered why they had put Deirdre *Briscoe* and not Deirdre Turner. She'd never been called Miss Briscoe in the neighbourhood, always Mrs Turner. It was very odd. Then he noticed the name of the newspaper in the corner. It wasn't a local paper, it was *The Times*. Why was this stranger snooping around with these things in his car, and having tea with Peter and his uncle?

Joe searched the rest of the glove compartment. He found a torch, a spare bulb, some fuses, several cassettes, a bunch of new plastic bags, and some parking receipts. There was nothing to say who the man was, or where he came from. He pushed everything back where he had found it.

His curiosity had been roused, and he looked around for somewhere to hide. Peter's garden was no good, because the only shrub was the one under the window, and that was too close for comfort. The house opposite had a small tree in the front garden with bushy foliage. He walked towards it, glancing round, then climbed up. There was a fork in the tree about two metres off the ground. He found he could stand comfortably without being seen from the house windows, but with a good aerial view of the light green sports car.

He hoped the man wasn't staying long.

Joe had been in the tree for barely five minutes when the man came out, waving goodbye to Peter's uncle. Peter was nowhere to be seen.

The man sat in his car under the light of a street lamp. As soon as the front door to number twenty-eight had closed, his movements quickened to the speed of lightning. He slipped a flat rectangular object from under his jacket, pushing it into the glove compartment. Then he took a crumpled handkerchief from his pocket and stuffed it into one of the plastic bags. The whole thing took only a few seconds.

The car drove off.

Joe, deep in thought, climbed down the tree.

"That man was watching the house this morning," said Peter. It was never easy talking to his uncle, but it seemed the right time to mention it.

It was the wrong time. With the closing of the front door, his uncle's bright conversation and glowing smiles switched off like a power cut.

"That *man*?" he said angrily. "Don't you mean *Mr Woods*?"

"Yes. He was watching the house."

"Don't be stupid."

"But he was. I saw him. He was sitting in his car, watching the house."

His uncle raised his voice, as if raising his voice made his argument better.

"He saw my new Business Transfer Agency sign, Peter. He called into the office to discuss business ideas."

"But, Uncle, he followed—"

"DON'T BE STUPID! People don't sit in cars watching the houses of complete strangers. At this moment, I've got visitors coming. So wash up these things and then make yourself scarce. *Understand*?"

Peter went back into the sitting-room to collect the tea tray. As always, his eyes were drawn to the mantelpiece. He half knew what to expect, but he still couldn't believe it when he saw it.

The picture of his mother was missing.

CHAPTER SIX

The Man on the Telephone

Peter was in no doubt who had stolen the photograph of his mother: Mr Woods. He wanted his uncle to know straight away, in spite of the angry reaction he'd had before, about Mr Woods watching the house.

He hurried into the kitchen to tell him, but heard sounds coming from the bathroom upstairs. He dumped the dishes in the sink and had started running the hot water when the front doorbell rang. His uncle shouted for him to go. Peter turned off the tap and went to answer it.

A man and a woman stood on the step, both in business suits, both carrying briefcases, both medium height, both slim.

"You must be Peter," said the woman, smiling. "Is your Uncle Len at home?"

Peter nodded and showed them into the sitting-room, glancing again at the empty space where his mother's photograph belonged. He looked round, making sure it hadn't fallen down, or been moved.

"Uncle will be down in a minute," he said, and went back to the washing-up. He heard his uncle swanning down the stairs, heard him go in and greet his visitors like long-lost friends.

Peter had just finished the washing-up when the door opened again and his uncle emerged saying, "I'll just get you that coffee."

He came into the kitchen and Peter took a deep breath. He didn't want to waste any time. He wanted to tell his uncle now.

"That Mr Woods has stolen Mum's photograph," he blurted out, keeping his voice low. "It was there when he came, but now it's gone."

His uncle pushed his face close to Peter's and spoke quietly, pronouncing every syllable clearly.

"I'm not interested in your stupid problems, do you understand? I've enough of my own. I'm in the middle of setting up a franchise that will make me a rich man, and I can't waste time on your imaginings."

"But it's gone . . ." Peter couldn't look into the staring eyes. Instead, he fixed on the weak chin and bad teeth. His uncle pushed the kitchen door closed behind him with his foot and raised his voice higher. Peter could feel little spots of liquid landing on his face from his uncle's wet lips.

"If you're *sick* or *injured* or *dying*, let me know, and I'll drop my important business meeting and phone for an ambulance. If you're *not* any of those three things, don't bother me. Understand?"

Peter felt infuriated, his face beginning to burn. He wanted to swear at his uncle and *tell* him he was ugly and disgusting and stupid, and that the man in the sports car *was* important. But he didn't. He knew from experience that answering back would only make things worse. Instead, he rubbed a hand across his face to wipe away the spit and said "Yes" in a meek voice.

His uncle seemed satisfied with his show of power and Peter's easy submission. He fixed his flat, cold eyes on Peter, his voice still raised.

"When I was your age I didn't go namby-pambying to my parents every time I was worried about something. I sorted it out myself. I thought if you'd half a brain in your skull you'd do the same. You're going to be out of here when you're eighteen. That means you haven't got many more years to think about being a man. And every time you run to me with stupid problems your brain's not working, is it?

And if your brain's not working *now*, you'll have *no* chance when you're out in the big, wide world on your own, will you? Got that?"

Peter couldn't bear the eyes any longer. He nodded, then turned and left the kitchen. As he climbed the stairs, he heard his uncle put the kettle on and return to the sitting-room. He heard the other voices murmuring.

"That's the way." The man's voice. "They'll never let go of the apron strings if you keep pampering them."

Then the woman's: "Remember he only lost his mother six weeks ago, Len. I think you're being too hard."

Peter couldn't see the look on Len's face through the door crack, but he knew what it would be like: smug and superior.

"Let's get back to these budgets, shall we?" he heard Len's voice rise again, as if he wanted Peter to overhear. "I didn't ask to look after the kid. He's never liked me, and I must say he's not my type, either. We didn't see each other much when Deirdre was alive, so why start now? As long as the kid's fed and clothed and got a roof over his head, what's the difference? He's still better off than being in an orphanage."

Then the woman spoke again: "I still think you should be more . . ." followed by a word Peter couldn't make out.

His uncle lowered his voice to a murmur, and Peter strained to listen.

"Frankly, I put the announcement of his mother's death in the nationals under her real name, hoping his father might see it, but he hasn't turned up yet."

Peter froze in horror as his uncle's normal voice droned on.

"Now, these budgets. I think it's reasonable to assume two new franchisees every month. Agreed? With each one increasing turnover at the rate of, say, eight per cent per month in the first year, and twenty per cent per annum after that, I think we can build in some decent salaries and company cars for ourselves at the outset . . ."

In a daze, Peter moved slowly up the stairs to his room.

He took out the scrapbook he kept hidden beneath his underclothes in the chest of drawers. Inside was a newspaper cutting from the local paper, five weeks old. He couldn't remember how many times he'd read it, but he read it again now with new understanding.

BRISCOE, Deirdre Ann. Died on 9th September after a short illness. Much loved by brother Len and son Peter (12). The funeral took place today (Thursday).

It had been an innocent enough announcement of his mother's death. But there had only been one problem – the same problem that Joe had hinted at when they'd found Peter's mother's birth certificate in the attic. Why had his uncle announced her death in the papers by her maiden name, *Briscoe*, when everyone locally knew her as Mrs Turner?

A conversation he'd had with his uncle in the early days drifted through his mind.

"Uncle?"

"What?"

"When you put mum's notice in the paper, why did you call her Deirdre Ann *Briscoe* when she was Deirdre *Turner*?"

His uncle's response played back in his head like a cassette tape, full of its usual patronising impatience.

"I put Briscoe in the paper because her *name* was Briscoe. Right? I'm her brother, so I think I should know, don't you? I don't know *why* she called herself Mrs Turner. She was Deirdre Briscoe, I'm Leonard Briscoe, and you're Peter Briscoe. What could be simpler to understand than that?"

"But she was married, wasn't she – once?"

In his mind's eye, he could still see his uncle's beady eyes expanding, swivelling on to him, sticking like leeches, clinging, sucking his confidence.

"No, she wasn't married. She never married. Not as far as I know. If she was married, you'd be called Peter Turner, wouldn't you, stupid?"

It had made Peter *feel* stupid, but he knew that he wasn't. He just wanted to know, that's all. He didn't know why he was called Peter Briscoe. He didn't know his mother never married, and he didn't know why she would have called herself Mrs Deirdre Turner if she wasn't. Especially when her real name was Deirdre Briscoe. It was his uncle who was stupid.

His uncle's final dismissal had been callous.

"Just one of life's little mysteries, I'm afraid," he'd said. "It's a great pity if it's cracked your little world apart, but you've got to learn to face these sort of things in life. You might as well start learning now, mightn't you? It's high time you started thinking for yourself, making your own decisions."

Now Peter knew he'd been lying, covering up the truth. He'd used the name Briscoe so Peter's father, if he saw it, would recognise it. *It meant his uncle had good reason to believe that Peter's father wasn't dead.*

Later that evening, when the two "business" associates had gone, there was another visitor. Peter watched from the darkness at the top of the stairs as his uncle led the new arrival into the sitting-room. He was short and square-jawed and, like most of his uncle's visitors, carried a briefcase. With the sitting-room door closed, Peter moved further down to pick up some of the conversation.

His uncle's voice, muted this time: "Are you *sure* there wasn't any other insurance, Mr Naylor?"

Then the visitor: "Nothing I was aware of. There was the endowment, so the mortgage has been cleared, as you know. When Peter was five, Mrs Turner set up the other policy in trust with Peter as beneficiary and yourself as trustee. You

59

had the cheque for that several weeks ago, of course. It speeds things up if they're written in trust, you see—"

Peter didn't understand many of the words, but he recognised his own name. He wasn't quite sure what a life policy was. He began to wonder if his mother had left him some money, after all. But she never had much to spare, so how could she have?

His uncle was interrupting.

"But there must have been *something* else. I've got a lot of expenses for that boy. I don't think the trust money is going to last very long."

"Well, I've been Mrs Turner's financial adviser from when she first bought this house. She did all her insurance business through me."

"Didn't she have any life cover through her employer's scheme?"

"They didn't have one. I rang them when the news came through, to check. But you've got the house, and Peter's trust money. Quite a decent sum, really."

"It is a *discretionary* trust, though?"

"Oh, yes."

"So the named beneficiaries are not necessarily those who might ultimately benefit . . .?"

"No. You've got the list of possible beneficiaries in the box there on the form."

"Ah, yes. Any child or grandchild, any beneficiary under the will of the deceased . . ."

The voices droned on.

Peter hadn't understood much of it at all – except that his uncle had been left the house, and there was some money for him, Peter. He felt pleased that his mother had planned everything properly. Even written him the letter. The money would probably be kept for him until he was eighteen, or twenty-one. He'd heard of trusts. It meant the money was put somewhere safe where no one could touch it.

He turned and crept back up the stairs to his room and quietly closed the door.

For the first time since he'd found the diary, he felt slightly happier again.

Later that night, Peter lay awake, staring at the shadows that hugged the corners of his ceiling.

He thought of how his life had turned upside down when his mother had died so suddenly. He hadn't been able to believe it at first. He'd hung by her bedside holding her limp hand, hoping, wishing, praying that she'd be all right.

At the end, she'd only opened her eyes once. She never said anything. He wasn't even sure she knew what was happening. Finally, his uncle was there. No tears in *his* eyes. Then soon, too soon, his mother had slipped away.

Since that day, his life had been a misery. He'd tried to get on with his uncle at first, but it was hopeless. Broken fragments of early conversations with his uncle drifted through his mind like bits of flotsam on a river.

"Oh, you want me to be your slave, do you? I'm busy enough in the mornings getting up early for work without making you cups of tea. It's you who should be getting up and making me a cup of tea, not the other way round . . ."

"You don't think I volunteered to look after you, do you? I enjoyed things just the way they were before I was lumbered with you. You're not the only one who's had to make adjustments . . ."

"Listen. The only reason I came to live with you and look after you was because your mother asked me to in her will. But don't think that means I'm going to fuss you, because I'm not . . ."

"If our sister in Canada hadn't been killed you might have gone to stay with her. Unfortunately for you and me, it wasn't to be . . ."

"You've already been spoilt, that's your trouble. Your

mother did everything you needed, and gave you everything you asked for, and now you're missing it. Well, get used to the idea that life is plain from now on. It's the only way you'll grow up tough and able to look after yourself. From tomorrow you can wash your own clothes and iron your own shirts . . ."

Now, his life had turned upside down again.

This morning, they had found the diary. Then the man in the green sports car had come, watching the house. Mr Woods. Following his uncle to find out where he worked. Why did he want to look in the house? Why was he so interested in the picture of his mother? Why had he tried to take a photo of it? And when he failed, why had he stolen it?

And now, the shocking news that his father might be alive somewhere, not dead. If his uncle thought so, it must be possible.

Peter suddenly remembered something else. The handkerchief. Why had Mr Woods been so keen to get hold of the dirty old hanky – especially horrible with Joe's blood on it?

And then Joe. Joe running off. What had Joe found that was so frightening that he wouldn't even show it to Peter?

Round and round. His head went round and round. The diary. *Today my poor baby Peter died.* Joe running off. *"Don't look at it!"* The man in the green sports car. *"Peter, I want you to meet Mr Woods."* Watching the house. Talking to Joe. Pumping Mrs Spinks. Trying to be nice and friendly. Really wanting to know about his mother. Asking about his father.

What did he want? *What did he want?*

Eventually, as Peter's thoughts tumbled over and over like socks in a washing machine, *the voice* came pushing through.

He listened in the silence. The voice draped itself around

him like a blanket, wrapping him in the strange words he couldn't really hear or understand. Calling him, yet not calling him. Calling someone else, someone he didn't know. Yet calling *him*.

Time passed and a gentle snore came from his uncle's room, but the voice still lingered. It prodded him – maddening, disturbing prods – yet it comforted him. It was the one thing in his life that hadn't changed. It had gone away for several years, but now that it had come back it was stronger. It warmed him like a log fire on a winter's evening. He couldn't tell whether it was male or female, old or young. But it knew him. It knew he was there.

As sleep surrounded him, the voice was calling for him to come.

Peter woke up with a jump. He'd been dreaming a lot, and none of the dreams had been pleasant. The last dream, which had started out being nice, had ended with him boasting loudly to Joe: "*I'm going to get lots of money when I'm grown up.*"

Joe's reply in the dream had startled him awake, filling him with a horrible dread.

"*If your uncle doesn't spend it all first.*"

Lying awake with his heart fluttering, Peter thought it was peculiar. Why would Joe say something like that – in a dream? But the more he thought about it, the more real it sounded. It was just like the sort of thing Joe *would* say.

For the first time, Peter began to wonder about other aspects of his uncle's behaviour. How had he bought his new car, when he'd always been in a low-paid job, living in a council flat? He thought of his uncle's wardrobe full of new suits, new clothes, new shoes. The new shaver wrapped in brown paper. How had he started his new business? Didn't you need lots of money to start a business? It couldn't have come from Peter's mother – she only had a few hundred pounds in the building society – Peter had seen the passbook lots of times.

He could hear his uncle moving about in the bedroom next door, and decided not to go downstairs until he had left for work. There was no point in mentioning his mother's missing picture again, or the behaviour of the man in the sports car. He couldn't bear the thought of more criticism and the dead-fish eyes.

"*Are you wearing that all day?*"

"*Why don't you put something decent on?*"

"*Spending the whole day lazing around as usual?*"

At half-past eight, he climbed out of bed.

"I'm going!" his uncle shouted a few minutes later. "I hope you're up!" The front door slammed.

Peter watched from his bedroom window. The same pompous stroll to the car, the same boastful flick of the wrist to unlock the fancy car with its ultrasound key, the same wobble of the head as he climbed in.

"Good riddance!"

As soon as his uncle had gone, Peter went down to the desk where all the family papers were kept. But before he had a chance to look at anything, the telephone rang. Peter picked it up, hoping it was Joe.

"Hello?"

Over a crisp, clear line, a man's gruff voice came through. It sounded like someone with a sore throat.

"May I speak to Peter Briscoe, please?"

Peter's heart lurched. It sounded like the sort of voice that was going to complain about something – him or Joe climbing over fences, perhaps, or – or anything.

"This is Peter Briscoe speaking."

"Hello, Peter." The gruff voice softened. "My name is Frank Pollard." The voice paused, as if waiting for some reaction from Peter. When none came, it went on. "Do you know who I am?"

"No," said Peter. "*And I don't particularly care, either,*" he said to himself.

"Oh." The man seemed disappointed. "Doesn't the name Frank Pollard mean anything to you at all?"

"No," said Peter.

"Didn't your mother ever mention me?"

"No." Peter started feeling uneasy. "What do you want?"

"Your mother *must* have mentioned me . . . Peter." The voice softened into a warm rasp. "Do you mind me calling you Peter?"

"Everyone else does." Peter began to think it was one of those weird phone calls. The best thing to do was to hang up. Even as he started moving the receiver away from his ear, he caught the next few words, and brought it back up again.

" – I'm sure your mother must have mentioned me, Peter. Can't you remember her mentioning Frank?"

"No." Even as he said it, Peter's heart nearly stopped. He *had* heard the name before – only yesterday. His mind raced back to the entry in the diary in the attic. "*Too fat to get into swimming costume. Frank swam and windsurfed.*" Frank. Frank swam. Frank windsurfed.

There was a pause. Then the voice continued still more quietly, almost like a purr. Peter knew what the words would be, before they came.

"*I'm your father.*"

CHAPTER SEVEN

Certificates

Even though Peter knew the words were coming, they still had the same devastating effect. He was suddenly dismayed and disoriented. He felt as if he'd been cracked on the head, or fallen giddy off a roundabout. He sat down on the telephone chair, shaking.

He must have been silent for a long time, because the voice on the other end, back to a warm rasp, kept saying, "Are you still there? Are you still there?"

In a silent daze, Peter put down the receiver. His head was still spinning when he picked it up again and, with shaking hands, tapped in Joe's number.

"Hello?"

"Hello, Mrs Robson. It's Peter. Is Joe there?"

"No, love. He's running an errand for me. Are you all right? Your voice is shaking."

"Yes. Can you tell him—"

"What, love? Tell him you called?"

"Oh – nothing. Just tell him – *to come round*. Please. Straight away. Thanks."

Peter had breakfast. It was like trying to eat cotton wool, his throat tight with fear and his head numb from the mad thoughts that buzzed round inside, swarming with doubt. Who was this man? Why would he telephone now? Why would he say he was his father if he wasn't? With every slow mouthful he glanced across at the phone, waiting for Joe to ring, needing his support. Almost as soon as he'd finished his cereal, the phone rang again. He grabbed it up, hoping it was Joe.

"Joe?"

"Peter?" It was the rasping voice again, not Joe. "Please don't hang up. It's Frank Pollard."

Peter stood soundless, his heart fluttering like a trapped butterfly against a window. He wanted to know who the man really was, why he was calling. If it was his father, why hadn't he ever rung before? Was it because his mother was gone? Was it because he knew she wasn't there to tell Peter what he was really like, this man? To tell him the truth?

"Peter? Please speak to me, Peter. I'm trying to help you."

Still Peter didn't answer.

Slowly, the voice at the other end tried again.

"Just listen, then, Peter, if you don't want to talk. I understand my phone call must have come as a big shock to you, but *I am your father*. It can be always be proved. DNA tests are all the rage. Do you know what DNA is?"

Still no answer.

"I never married your mother – I'm sorry I didn't. But I never married anyone else, either. So you're my only son, and I want you to come to my house and meet me and have a talk. I'm a rich man, Peter. I've got all the money I need. I want to share it with you, Peter. I—"

Peter replaced the receiver.

He stood motionless for a second, then went through to the bookshelf in the sitting-room. He looked along the row at the *Children's Encyclopaedia*, the World Atlas, the dictionary. His mother always encouraged him to look things up for himself. He chose the last fat volume, pulled it out, solid and heavy, and slapped it on to the coffee table. He thumbed from the front, Arctic, Bedlam, Bronchitis, Domo, too far. Back one page. "*D.N.A.* abbr *deoxyribonucleic acid, the self-replicating material present in most living organisms that carries the genetic information necessary for reproducing life.*"

Peter replaced the dictionary and pulled out the third volume of the encyclopaedia.

"The structure of DNA was discovered by James Watson and Francis Crick. In the 1980s and beyond it was used more and more in the detection of crime, by matching the DNA found at the scene of a crime (in skin, hair, blood etc) with that of a suspect. The technique, like fingerprinting, has only a one-hundred-million-to-one chance of being identical in two human beings. DNA tests can also be used to determine whether a child is the biological issue of a parent."

Peter read it twice over, then the doorbell rang.

It was Joe.

"Joe! Why did you run off like that? I tried to ring you. . ."

Joe, not looking his usual jokey self, stepped inside.

"Joe! Tell me! *What did you find? Why did you take it away?*" Peter half-pulled him inside, slammed the front door, bolted it, pulled the curtain across.

"Never mind that," said Joe, grimly. "I came back last night and watched that bloke in the sports car. Who is he?"

"I don't know," Peter said, almost desperate. "There's really strange things happening, Joe . . ."

"I know. . ."

"What's going on? Why did you run off yesterday? *Show me what you found!*"

"I told you. *Never mind about yesterday.* It's what happened last night you should worry about!"

"Why? What happened?"

"I had a look in that man's sports car. I couldn't believe it when I looked through your window and saw you having tea with him – not that you looked too happy – why was he in your house, anyway?"

"Never mind why he was in the house. What did you find in his car?"

"A piece of paper with *your mum's name* written on it,

only it called her *Caroline* Turner.

Peter frowned.

"Her *sister* was called Caroline. My aunt. She used to live in Canada, but she's dead now. What else?"

"There was a newspaper cutting about the death of Miss Deirdre *Briscoe*, and a map book with *your road* circled on it!"

Peter stared.

"Something else strange happened," he said.

"What?"

"Someone telephoned."

"Who?"

Peter looked away.

"Someone called Frank Pollard. *He said he was my father.*"

It was Joe's turn to look stunned.

"What?!"

Peter told Joe everything that had happened since the day before, and Joe told Peter what he'd seen when Mr Woods went back to his car.

"That makes it definite, then," said Peter. "That rectangular thing was the photograph of my mum."

"Why did you give him that?"

"I didn't *give* it to him, he *stole* it."

"Why?"

"I don't know. And he took my hanky as well – the one with your blood on it. It was really odd."

Peter told him about the other visitors and the insurance man, and finally the telephone calls from the man claiming to be his father.

"If the phone rings again, *you* can answer it," Peter finished.

Then he led Joe to the desk in the sitting-room.

"Come on. There's things in here we can look at."

Peter opened the biggest drawer and pulled out a file that

was lying flat inside. He stood it upright and fanned it open like a concertina, showing pockets labelled with the letters of the alphabet.

"This is where Mum kept her papers," he said. "I used to file things for her sometimes. "If it was water rates, I'd file it under 'W', if it was a gas bill I'd file it under - "

"G," interrupted Joe. "Yes, I get the general idea. What are we looking for?"

"Anything. Mum's marriage certificate, for one thing. So we can see who Mr Turner was."

Good idea," said Joe. "Let's start at 'A' and work through. We can take it in turns again."

"Not much under 'A'," said Peter, pulling out a small wad of papers. "Just one of her credit card accounts." He shoved the sheets back, and Joe delved into "B".

"A building society book," said Joe. He opened it and looked inside. "Account closed," he read. "About two weeks ago."

"How much was in there?"

"Three hundred and sixty-two pounds forty-seven pence. That's funny."

"What?"

"It says 'Mrs C Turner' – like it did in that man's car. "Shouldn't it be 'D' for Deirdre?"

"Perhaps it was her husband's initial – women use that sometimes with 'Mrs'."

"In the man's car, it said *Caroline*."

"Let's look at the credit card thing again," said Peter. He pulled them out and looked at the name. "Mrs *Caroline* Turner," he read. "I didn't notice that before."

"You said you used to file things. Didn't you ever ask her?"

"I just never thought anything. She liked to be called 'Deirdre', that's all. Lots of people call themselves by different names – not always their real one."

"But Deirdre was her real name," Joe reminded him. "It said so on her birth certificate in the attic."

Peter shrugged.

"I know it's peculiar. That's why we're looking, isn't it?" From "C" he pulled out a brown envelope labelled "Certificates". He emptied the contents and looked at them, handing them to Joe one by one. The first was his own birth certificate, stiffish and new.

Peter John Briscoe. Born 25th October. Mother: Deirdre Ann Briscoe. Father: Unknown.

"Look," said Joe. "It says your mother is *Deirdre Ann*, not Caroline. It doesn't make sense.

"And look," said Peter, "there's no name for my father – he's unknown."

"How can he be unknown?" said Joe. "Surely she must have—"

"It's not that," said Peter. "She always said he wasn't worth talking about."

"He obviously wasn't worth writing about, either," Joe muttered.

Peter handed over another birth certificate.

Caroline Helen Briscoe. Born 12th June. Mother: Caroline Primrose Briscoe. Father: Peter Henry Briscoe.

"That isn't my mum's birthday," said Peter. "My mum's birthday was on the 10th February – like the one in the attic said. That one had the right year, as well. This one's five years too early. This must be my *aunt's* birth certificate – the one who died in Canada."

Just then the telephone rang, and Peter froze.

"You answer it," he said.

Joe went into the kitchen and picked up the receiver. Peter

71

stayed by the desk, listening.

"Hello?" he heard Joe say. "Yes, he is . . . No, you can't . . . And he says if you don't stop making nuisance phone calls he'll tell the police."

"Joe!"

Joe banged the phone down and came back, grinning.

"Was that him?"

Joe nodded.

"That'll teach him," he said.

The next certificate was for Peter's Uncle Len, and the last was for a marriage between Caroline Helen Briscoe, spinster, and Mark Handford Turner, bachelor.

"That's my aunt getting married to Mr Turner," said Peter, "two years before I was born. But my aunt was married to a man called Raymond. Copeland, I think their name was. They both died in a car crash a few years ago. None of it makes sense."

"Perhaps your mum married before you were born, divorced, and went back to her single name?" said Joe, weakly.

"But my mum was *Deirdre. Deirdre Ann*!"

They went through everything else in the desk, and the story was the same whatever they looked at. Everything to do with Peter's mother was in the name Caroline H Turner.

Under the letter "I" they found insurance papers, including a photocopy of an application form. It was dated around Peter's fifth birthday, and was again in the name Caroline Helen Turner. It was a life assurance for lots of money, and there were copies of other forms attached. Under the word "Trustee" there was a box with the name Leonard Spencer Briscoe, with his signature and his old address. Another box was headed "Beneficiaries" and had Peter's name in it and "100%".

There was nothing else in the file that told them anything new.

"I'll ask my mum," said Joe, suddenly.

Peter looked concerned.

"Don't tell her anything about this," he said.

"I won't," said Joe. "Don't worry."

"Mum?"

"Yes, love."

"Why do people change their names?"

"All sorts of reasons. Sometimes they don't like the name they've got."

"Any other reasons?"

Mrs Robson considered.

"If you were married to someone and then divorced you might want to change back to your single name."

"Yeah, I know about that one. Any more?"

"You're very curious all of a sudden," said Mrs Robson suspiciously. "You're not thinking of changing yours, are you?"

"No. I like being Joe."

"Why do you want to know, then?"

"I just do, that's all."

Joe's older brother, who had been listening in the next room, couldn't stand being left out any longer and came strolling in.

"You might want to change your identity so you can't be found," he said.

"Who might? Criminals?"

"Yes, criminals. Any people who want to start a new life. People who want to hide from their relatives. People who owe money and don't want to be found. All sorts of reasons. People who are ashamed of something and can't face their old friends."

"How do you change your name?" said Joe.

"Officially, by Deed Poll."

"What's that?"

73

His brother was getting on to stony ground.

"Er . . . it's an official sort of paper, and it's called a Deed Poll – that's all I know. It tells everyone you've changed your name officially."

"Or if you get married," said Mrs Robson, "the woman's name usually changes – unless she's someone famous. She might keep her old name, then."

"What if you didn't want anyone to know you'd changed it?" said Joe.

"Well," his mother continued, "you can just call yourself something different. You can call yourself Adolf Hitler if you want to. There's nothing to stop you. The trouble comes if you want a passport or a driving licence. You have to prove who you are, then, and that means producing a birth certificate with your name on it."

"And a Deed Poll if you've changed it," said his brother. "Or a marriage certificate, if you're a married woman."

"What do they do, then?" said Joe. "People who are hiding, I mean. How do they get licences and things if they've changed their name?"

"If they're criminals," said his brother, "they'd probably get forgeries made. Sometimes people are actually hidden by the police. They're given new identities and false certificates and passport and everything. People who've been fighting terrorists and need to disappear in case of reprisals – that sort of thing."

"So," said Joe, slowly, "if a woman wanted to hide away – so no one she knew could find her – she could just get married and change her name that way?"

"That's a good way. There'd be a marriage certificate, then."

"What if they borrowed someone else's?"

"That's happened before. It has been known for people to use certificates belonging to dead people. It only causes complications if someone happens to look up the death records. What's all this about, anyway?"

"Just curiosity," said Joe, then disappeared hastily before they could probe any further.

"I've got it!" said Joe.

He was on Peter's doorstep again, and Peter ushered him inside.

"Got what?"

"The answer."

"Which one?"

Joe looked exasperated.

"Why your mum called herself Mrs Turner, of course."

"Why did she?"

"So she could hide from your father, I reckon. Don't you see? He'd be looking for her as *Deirdre Briscoe*, but she'd be down in any records as *Caroline Turner*. He'd never find her, not in any phone books, or anywhere."

"But how could she just—"

"The next bit's a guess," said Joe. "Her sister's gone to Canada, right?"

"Yes."

"And got married. Right?"

"Yes."

"To Raymond Copeland, yeah?"

"Yes."

"*But what if she was married before?*"

"Well, she was. . ."

"That's right. We saw the certificate. Your aunt married this Mr Turner a few years before you were born, and then divorced him, or he died, or something . . ."

"I still don't see . . ."

"It's easy. Your mum would be able to borrow her *sister's* birth certificate *and* her *first* marriage certificate. There wouldn't be a real Mrs Turner any more. Her sister was Mrs Copeland by then, and she was out of the way in Canada."

"You're saying my mum stole them?"

Joe considered.

"Not necessarily. Your aunt might have said okay. Your mum probably told your aunt she wanted to hide from your dad. That makes sense, doesn't it?"

Peter thought about it.

"I suppose it does."

"And don't you see? *That would explain why your mum's real birth certificate was in the dusty box in the attic*! She wouldn't be needing it ever again!"

"Okay," said Peter slowly, "But—"

"But what?"

"I dunno. I dunno what happens next. I dunno where we are or who I am."

"What about this man who says he's your father?" said Joe.

Peter stared at Joe.

"But he *can't* be my father, can he?"

Joe tried to look blank as he stared back at Peter's serious, worried face.

"What do you mean?"

"You know what I mean. You're just being thick on purpose. The diary. Remember? *Today my poor baby Peter died*. That means whoever Peter *was*, this Frank Pollard might have been *his* father, but he's not mine. I don't know *who* I am. I'm somebody else, aren't I?"

Peter stared straight into Joe's eyes, but Joe looked away.

"Aren't I?" Peter repeated.

Joe glanced up and found Peter still staring at him. He looked down again hastily, thinking hard, trying to decide something. Then slowly, very slowly, he reached inside his shirt front and pulled out a piece of paper that had been folded into three.

"Is that what you found in the attic?" said Peter.

Joe pushed the piece of paper towards his friend. "You

might as well have a look at it. I wasn't going to show it to you, but I suppose you ought to see it now."

Peter took it and opened the two folds. As he spun it round on the desk nearby, he could already see the fancy words at the top: "*Certificate of Death*".

His eyes misted over as he read the scrawly writing underneath:

> *Name of deceased: Peter John Briscoe;*
> *Born: 25th October;*
> *Died: 26th October;*
> *Cause of Death: Myocardial Infarction.*

"I don't know who you are, either," said Joe. "But one thing's certain. *You're not Peter Briscoe.*"

CHAPTER EIGHT

Invitation

Peter read the certificate again, blinking away the mist in his eyes. In that moment, he felt horribly alone. Isolated. It was as if everything he had ever known had been wrenched away from him. If the real Peter Briscoe had died the day after he was born, who was he, the boy who *thought* he was Peter Briscoe? Suddenly the earth itself seemed like an alien place. He felt like a stranger, an astronaut, looking down at the earth from a spaceship, watching it get smaller and further away, knowing that the spaceship was faulty, and that he could never return or be rescued. The earth would shrink to a pinpoint of light, and he would be lost forever in a black void. He felt dark desolation creeping over him.

With a huge effort, he forced his mind back to his mother's letter, felt its comforting edge inside his shirt. *Be brave and grow honest and strong.* At last he understood why Joe hadn't wanted him to see what he had found: the certificate of his own death.

Joe spoke softly, mirroring his thoughts.

"Now you know why I didn't want you to see it," he said.

Peter stared at the paper for another few seconds, then thrust it back at Joe. He closed his eyes, then opened them again, staring at his friend. At least Joe was the same. At least Joe hadn't changed.

He took a deep breath and tried to compose himself. *Find it in your heart to forgive me. . .*

When at last he spoke, his voice came out broken and odd.

"You'd better put it somewhere safe. I wouldn't want Uncle Len to see it. Or anyone else. You won't tell anyone, will you?"

"Of course I won't."

"It's horrible, isn't it?"

"We've got to find out who you *really* are. That's what we've got to do. And when we've found out, *then* we'll tell 'em."

"How can we find out?"

"Well, the first thing you can do is to go and see this Frank Pollard who thinks he's your father. I mean, he might have been Peter Briscoe's father, but we know now – he's not yours, is he?"

"What's the point of seeing him, then? How's that going to help?"

"Well, he must know about your mother, mustn't he?"

"I still don't see . . ."

Joe raised his voice, as if hoping it might penetrate Peter's brain better that way.

"You want *clues*, dumb head! You've got to start *somewhere*, haven't you? Why not start with him? He knew your mother, didn't he?"

"Yes, I . . . I suppose so."

"Great! There's a good start, then. Who else knew your mum in the early days?"

"I don't know. My uncle Len – and he never tells me anything, or if he does it's just lies – and my Aunt Caroline, but she's dead.

"So it looks like Mr Pollard, then, doesn't it?"

"There's only one problem," said Peter.

"What?"

"You told him to get lost, and I haven't got his phone number."

Joe shrugged it off.

"If he really thinks he's your father, you don't think he'll give up that easily, do you?"

*

Peter's doubts re-surfaced as soon as Joe had gone back home for lunch. He wanted to meet this man who claimed to be his father, but he was afraid. He wanted to find out if he knew anything about his mother, or himself, but the events of the last few days had left him with a bad feeling in his stomach. What had Frank Pollard done that had made his mother run away? What was so terrible that she would move such a long way away, and go to all that trouble to change her name? Something in Peter's mind told him that it must have been a lot worse than an ordinary quarrel.

And then there was Mr Woods. He'd been watching the house. Why had he done that? Why had he tried to see Peter when his uncle was at work? Why had he taken his mother's photograph off the mantelpiece, and the handkerchief?

The more Peter thought about things, the more suspicious everything looked. Why had Frank Pollard suddenly made contact, after all these years, almost as soon as his mother had died? Had he been waiting just for that?

Peter didn't know why, but all his instincts were telling him to be cautious. Something else – he didn't know what – was telling him that the answer to everything lay inside the box in the attic. Whatever happened, he had to guard that box until he discovered its secret. He certainly couldn't go away and risk leaving it for someone else to find.

For half an hour he agonised, tumbling the thoughts over and over in his mind as he had done the night before.

He wondered who he really was, and what would become of him.

When Joe didn't come back after lunch, Peter went into the attic again. He dragged the box out, took it down to his bedroom, and looked at everything once more. There was still nothing else that seemed to help.

He decided to take the box to Joe's and get Joe to hide it somewhere.

He split two plastic carrier bags, taped them round the box, and set off. Joe's mother answered the door.

"Hello, Mrs Robson."

"Hello, Peter."

"Is Joe in?"

"No, love. He's helping his father in the back of the shop this afternoon. Didn't he tell you?"

"No."

"Knowing Joe, he probably forgot about it himself," Mrs Robson went on. "Now I think about it, it did seem to come as a bit of a complete surprise to him at lunch-time, in spite of me reminding him twice at breakfast."

"Oh. So he won't be back until this evening?"

"No, love."

"Can I leave this for him, then, please?"

"Course you can." Joe's mother took the package. "Any message?"

"Yes. Just tell him . . . to guard it with his life – and not to tell anyone he's got it."

Joe's mother gave him a withering look.

"Guard it with his life . . ." she repeated, raising her eyebrows. "Right . . ."

Peter thanked her and retraced his steps. He felt much happier with the box out of the way. If Mr Woods did any more snooping, at least he wouldn't find the box – not that there seemed to be anything very secret in it, apart from the diary.

As soon as Peter reached his house again, he felt odd. He couldn't shake off the feeling that forces of evil were tightening around him like the tentacles of some awful monster.

The first sign was on the mat. It was a letter without a stamp on, hand-delivered and hand-written with the words "Master Peter Briscoe" on the envelope.

With his hands shaking, Peter ripped it open and read the letter inside. It was headed "PASSMEADOW HALL" and written in the same neat hand:

Dear Peter,
Here is my address and telephone number, to show you I'm
not just a stranger. I'm afraid I haven't got anything to send
you to prove that I'm your father, I never had a photograph
of your mother, and I don't think she ever had one of me. I'll
telephone again in the hope that you'll talk to me.
Yours,
Frank Pollard.

There was another envelope tucked inside the letter. Inside it were two brand-new £50 notes. Peter could hardly believe his eyes. He passed the notes through his hands, feeling their lovely crispness, then pushed them carefully into the back pocket of his jeans.

He wondered what his uncle would say if he saw the letter. He tried to imagine the mostly one-sided conversation, and it wasn't difficult. He could hear his uncle's voice in his head as if he was there in front of him, spraying spit and raising his voice because he thought it made him sound more intelligent:

"Good. So he's turned up, then. Funny we all thought he
was dead, wasn't it? That's what your mother told us, that's
the trouble. On the other hand, this could be from a crank.
We'll give it to the police, shall we, and let them sort him
out?"

"But I want to go and see him. Isn't that why you announced Mum's death in all the papers? So I could see him?"

"So you don't think I'm good enough for you? Well, at
least you'd be off my hands, then. It's up to you if you want
to live with a complete stranger. The man might be

dangerous. Why do you think Deirdre ran away? You know nothing about him at all, except that he drove your mother out."

Then Peter could hear himself trying to explain why it was important, and failing, not being able to give any of the reasons.

"But, uncle, you don't understand. You see, I'm not really Peter B—"

No. He couldn't tell his uncle anything. He didn't *want* to tell his uncle anything. He didn't want his uncle to know that he wasn't really Peter Briscoe. He didn't want him to know that the real Peter Briscoe was dead, and he didn't want him to know anything else. It was *his* secret, between himself and his mother. The only thing he had left to share with her. Not Uncle Len. If she'd wanted Len to know, she would have told him. Otherwise, why had the solicitor given Peter the letter from his mother in secret? *So no one else would know!*

That evening, emboldened by his secret, Peter felt calm and confident enough to tackle his uncle. It wasn't a feeling he had ever had before, and he hoped it wouldn't go badly wrong. They were having tea in silence when Peter dropped his question into the air.

"Uncle . . . what would happen if my real father turned up? Would you still be the one to look after me, or would he have to?"

"He can't. He's dead."

"But suppose he wasn't? Mum never said who he was, did she? Perhaps she only used to tell everyone he was dead because she didn't want him to find me?"

"Look. He's dead. Your mother said he was dead, and that's good enough for me. Okay? So stop dreaming and do something useful to prepare yourself for life. There's my shirts to iron for one thing. I'm not giving you a pound a week pocket money for nothing, you know. You've got to earn your keep in this house."

Peter felt strangely comforted. True to form, his uncle's lies had ended with a little lecture, more abrupt than usual.

He looked across the table. His uncle's dead-fish eyes told him that he had already gone back to dreaming big business.

That night, as Peter lay in bed, and the clock ticked in the hall downstairs, and the world slowed down to a gentle hum, the voice came again. This time it was so strong and so real he knew he had a mission to follow. He didn't know where the trail would lead, or what he would find at the end of it. But the voice in his head was so compelling, it pulled at his will like a magnet, drawing him on. It didn't have direction, or distance, or focus – only a compulsion that knew he was there, and spoke to him in words and language that he didn't understand. He didn't know whether the voice was good or evil, or mad or sane, and he didn't care. He only knew that it motivated and comforted him. That was all that mattered. He didn't even know if he was mad or sane himself, but that didn't seem to matter, either.

By the time he woke up suddenly at six o'clock the following morning, he already knew what he was going to do.

Feeling happier, he dozed off again, but when he woke up at a quarter to seven, his uncle was standing over his bed holding two crisp £50 notes in his hand.

"*Where did you get these?*"

Peter opened his eyes wider, trying to think, realised with horror that his uncle had somehow found the money that Frank Pollard had sent him. As Peter pretended to wake up slowly and come to his senses he realised what a stupid mistake he'd made. He'd dropped his jeans untidily on the floor when he'd gone to bed, and the money must have been sticking out of the pocket. Uncle Len must have passed his door and seen it.

"What are they?" said Peter at last, trying to buy some time.

"You know perfectly well what they are. They're £50 notes. New ones."

"Oh, those," said Peter. "I got them out of my savings account."

"*Let me see your account book.*"

Peter knew it wouldn't work. He struggled to think of something else.

"No . . . not mine. I mean *Joe* got them out of his savings account. He asked me to look after them."

"Peter, you're lying to me. I don't know why you're lying to me, and I don't know why you've got a hundred pounds in your jeans pocket. If you did take it from your savings account, I'd like to know exactly why you want a hundred pounds right now. Are you going to explain?"

Peter had run out of ideas. He just felt thankful that he hadn't left the letter from Frank Pollard in the same pocket.

When Peter's silence had extended to several seconds, his uncle pushed the money into his own pocket.

"Well, I'll hang on to this, then, until you can give me a proper explanation," he said. He turned and went downstairs.

Peter stayed in bed until his uncle had gone to work. As soon as the door banged, he sprang to life, his mind made up.

He didn't want to take a rucksack – it would be too obvious – the same with a suitcase or a hold-all. He decided instead on a carrier bag. He didn't need much. Two changes of underclothes and socks, a few T-shirts, a spare pair of jeans, a toothbrush, toothpaste and comb. And money. All his money. He didn't know if it would be enough to get to where Frank Pollard lived, but he didn't care. He'd walk if he had to.

Someone would have to know where he'd gone, in case

anything went wrong. He'd tell Joe.

When his carrier bag was packed he went downstairs, had breakfast, then picked up the telephone.

"Mrs Robson? Is Joe there?"

"Sorry, love, he's been at the shop since early this morning. He won't be off till ten."

"Oh. Never mind, then."

"Can I give him a message?"

"No. It's okay, thanks. Bye."

Peter replaced the telephone, took Frank Pollard's letter from his breast pocket, and dialled the number. He heard the ringing tone and waited. A man's voice answered.

"Hello."

"Hello. May I speak to Mr Pollard, please?"

"May I say who's calling?"

"Peter Briscoe."

There was a pause and a click, then the gruff voice of Frank Pollard came on the line.

"Hello? Peter?"

"I got your letter," said Peter.

"Good. I was just about to ring you."

"I wondered if it would be all right to come and see you?"

There was a long pause. When the voice spoke again it was huskier, breaking up.

"Of course, Peter. That's what I want you to do. That's why I was going to telephone. When do you want to come?"

"Now. I'd like to come now, please."

"That's good. That's perfect. Does your uncle know I've spoken to you?"

"No."

"I should have spoken to him myself, really, shouldn't I?"

"I don't want him to know."

"Why not?"

"Because I'm running away."

There was another, longer, silence.

"Do you think that's a good idea, Peter?" Mr Pollard's voice came at last, hushed now. "If you run away, your uncle will be worried."

"He won't care. I don't care, either."

"You'd be a missing person, Peter. The police would be involved."

There was another pause, from Peter this time. Something wrong. Something out of place.

"How did you know I was living with my uncle?" he said suddenly.

The question was brushed aside.

"I'll tell you when I see you. Fair enough?"

"Okay. I'll leave a note, saying I've gone to find my father."

"Yes, you could, but it would be better if you got his permission first."

"He wouldn't let me come."

"Why not?"

"I don't know. I think he thinks you're dead, but I'm not really sure now."

"How about coming for the day?" Mr Pollard suggested. "You wouldn't have to run away, then, would you?"

"It's too far."

"I've already arranged something, Peter – hoping you'd say yes. There's a car coming to collect you, and bring you back before your uncle gets home. It's less than a hundred miles. Two hours here, two hours back. Here for lunch and home for tea. How about it?"

Peter felt relieved. This way, his uncle needn't be told anything. There was the hundred pounds to explain, that was all. Peter would have seen Frank Pollard by that time, so his uncle would be too late to stop him, then. The truth about the £50 notes wouldn't matter.

"As it's only for the day, can I bring Joe?"

"Who's Joe?"

"My friend."

"Of course you can, Peter. I'll call the Rolls now. The chauffeur's name is Norman. He'll pick you up soon."

"Can you make it ten o'clock, please. And not from my house. We've got a nosy neighbour."

"Where from, then?"

"There's a petrol station at the end of the High Street."

"Okay. And Peter—"

"Yes?"

"I'm looking forward to meeting you – after all these years."

"So am I. Goodbye."

Peter put the phone down. It had been easier than he'd thought. He was getting a free lift. He wouldn't have to spend his own money, and he wouldn't have to leave a note for his uncle.

Then the doubts set in again. He was being completely stupid. He was going in a strange car to see a complete stranger who had a mysterious past . . . He was breaking all the rules he'd ever been taught by his mother. He'd have Joe with him, but it was still stupid and dangerous, and yet . . . He knew what he'd do. He'd leave the letter with Frank Pollard's address under his pillow. His uncle would never look there, normally, but at least if Peter was murdered he'd find it eventually . . .

Peter decided he wouldn't need his carrier bag after all, and unpacked everything again. Then he went down to the shop where Joe was working and found Mr Robson behind the counter.

"Is Joe here, Mr Robson?"

"He's out the back, stacking a delivery. Shouldn't be long."

"Is it all right if I go through?"

"Of course. Help him if you like."

Peter approached Joe, dropping his voice to a whisper.

"Do you want a day out?"

Joe turned and grinned.

"Where?"

"To see Frank Pollard."

Joe didn't answer at first, just looked at Peter wide-eyed.

"Okay," he said at last. His eyes roamed the shelves, then came back to Peter. There was excitement in his voice. "But I've got something to show you. Something I found."

"In the box?"

"Yes."

"What? Can you tell me now?"

"No. It's too awkward. We'll have to be alone – really alone."

Peter judged from the tone of Joe's voice, and the look in Joe's eyes, that it was something really important. Like the death certificate.

He felt a surge of adrenalin running through his body, but he didn't press Joe any further.

CHAPTER NINE

Passmeadow Hall

Peter felt so excited about Joe's news that he found it difficult to stop his hands trembling. He told Joe the plan of action as he helped him stack the shelves.

Ten o'clock approached and they still hadn't finished, but Peter couldn't wait to see if the car had arrived. He hurried out, with Joe promising to follow as soon as he could.

Peter felt even more frightened when he saw that the car was really there, a big silver Rolls Royce in the far corner of the filling station. A uniformed chauffeur stood beside it, and raised his peaked cap as Peter approached.

"Master Peter Briscoe?" he said. His voice was flat and uninteresting.

Peter nodded.

"I'm Norman, Mr Pollard's chauffeur. Is your friend coming?"

"He'll be here in a few minutes."

"Would you like to sit in the car?"

Peter still felt cautious. He had deep-rooted fears of being locked in, hijacked, driven off without Joe. Apart from that, Joe's news of finding something in the box was burning a hole in his curiosity, and he wanted to see Joe in private before the journey began.

"No, thanks, I'll wait where Joe can see me."

He went back to the corner nearest the shop and waited. Five minutes later, Joe appeared in the distance. Peter hurried towards him.

"We won't be able to talk in the car," he said, excited. "I'm dying to know what you found?"

"I can't show you now," said Joe, more serious than usual. "It's stuffed inside my shirt, and we'll need to be really alone – trust me."

"Can't you even give me a clue?"

"You'll understand when I show you."

Further appeals were useless, and Peter had to be content with Joe's caution. He introduced him to Norman and climbed into the back seat of the Rolls, already half in a dream from the speed of strange events. Nothing seemed real any more. Inside, the car was more like a sitting-room than a car, with a television, music centre and drinks cabinet lined with fizzy drinks. Peter sat in a dazed silence while Joe played with the electric windows, opening and closing them, making them dance up and down.

He heard Norman's flat voice saying, "So you're the long lost Peter, are you?" and himself answering "Yes" as they turned on to the main road. He heard him using the telephone, saying, "We're on our way," and chatting on about nothing in particular.

Now Joe had switched on the television and was flicking through the channels. Peter was dimly aware of politicians talking, then an Indian film. He heard Joe mutter and give up, turn on the music centre, fail to find any music he liked, and turn it off again.

The car swished on as Joe tried everything in the drinks cabinet, all in one glass. Peter was aware of him saying it tasted odd, and some time later, Joe asking Norman to stop at the next public toilets.

Peter stayed balanced on the edge of sleep for most of the journey, his mind chasing thoughts that scattered like sheep on a hillside, fanning out in front of him, never quite within reach. As Joe experimented with the air-conditioning, blowing hot air to make a tropical rainforest, then cold to try freezing his drink, the voice in Peter's head came swimming in and out, weaving through his semi-consciousness. It was

91

like music this time, random notes and rhythms that didn't exist in real music. It was like an alien tune played on impossible instruments in another dimension.

After ninety minutes, the car turned off the main road. It purred for several miles along wooded lanes, and Peter became fully conscious when Norman announced that they had arrived. The car swung between two stone pillars with a sign that said, PASSMEADOW HALL.

They swept down a long, dusty drive between rhododendrons. After a hundred metres the shrubbery opened out, and Passmeadow Hall itself came into view. It was a huge Victorian house, surrounded by trees and paddocks. There was a row of garages on the left, with a Porsche and two less expensive cars parked outside.

Peter and Joe were escorted towards the huge oak front door. Norman pulled the bell and Peter heard it clang in the distance inside. At last the door opened, and an elderly man with wispy grey hair appeared. He stood majestically, peering down his nose at Peter and Joe with a hint of welcome.

"Mr Peter, I presume?" he said. "And Mr Joe?" His voice was rusty, like a hinge that hadn't been oiled since Victorian times.

"I'm Peter. This is Joe."

"My name is Havis," said the man. "Mr Pollard's butler. Do come in."

Peter stepped inside, with Joe close behind.

"Please follow me," said Havis. He turned and led the way up a wide staircase, which split into two after the first landing. He paused.

"I'm afraid Mr Pollard is otherwise engaged at the moment. He would naturally like to see you on your own first, Mr Peter, if that's acceptable."

"I don't mind."

Peter and Joe exchanged glances.

They were led off to the right, along a corridor and into a room on the left. Havis pushed at the solid oak door. Beyond it was a huge panelled room with a four-poster bed, a large antique desk, a television, video recorder, computer, and a multitude of soft chairs.

"Please be kind enough to wait here. I'll call you as soon as Mr Pollard is ready. In the meantime, Mr Pollard has given me strict instructions to look after you personally, and to make sure you have every comfort."

"Should I call you Mr Havis?"

"I would prefer just Havis, please, Mr Peter."

"Will Mr Pollard be long?"

"Business is a constant commitment. Delays are frequent."

Peter was still in a daze with the speed at which everything was happening, and still aching to know what Joe had found. Joe wandered over to the desk.

"Can we use this computer?" he asked.

"Oh, yes, sir. Mr Pollard knows that most children like computers. I believe you will find several games on it. Do you know how to operate it?"

"I can find out."

"I'm afraid computers are something of a mystery to me, Mr Joe. I never really had the chance to use one."

With that, Havis withdrew from the room, saying he'd be back in a moment. Joe switched on the computer.

As soon as Havis had gone, Peter went to Joe and gripped his arm, imploring him.

"Now, Joe!"

But Joe had already started tapping at the computer keyboard. As he typed, Peter read the words on the screen:

"DON'T SAY ANYTHING YET. WE DON'T KNOW WHO'S LISTENING. WHAT I'VE FOUND IS DANGEROUS."

Peter's shocked expression and dazed answering nod gave Joe the signal to erase the words. Then Joe said aloud, cheerfully, "Do you fancy a game?" He pointed at the menu.

"That's a good one. Armageddon."

Peter sat down to play the game with Joe, but found it impossible to concentrate. His mind was locked on to Joe's typed message, long faded from the screen: *What I've found is dangerous*. Why dangerous? How could it be *dangerous*?

They played in silence for a few minutes until Havis returned and sat down in one of the chairs behind them.

"Your father *is* anxious to meet you, Mr Peter – and will do so when he has finished his telephone conversation."

Peter turned to him.

"Is Mr Pollard a millionaire, Havis?"

"Oh yes, sir."

"What sort of business is it?"

"Oh – he, he buys and sells expensive goods on the international market. I think he's anxious for you to start enjoying the, er – the life-style – of a millionaire's son."

"But he doesn't even know me. I might be horrible."

"You are his only son, Mr Peter. He never married and has no other children. And he's spent a fortune looking for you."

"Really?"

"A *lot* of money."

"How much? Hundreds of pounds?"

"I believe the latest estimate is over fifty thousand pounds, sir."

"What!"

"Oh yes. He has hired dozens of private detectives over the years – the latest being Mr Woods, of course."

Peter and Joe stared, appalled. More pieces of the jigsaw were slowly slotting into place.

"Mr Woods?"

"Sir?"

"Did you say *Mr Woods* is a private detective?"

"Of course, sir." Then: "Oh, dear, have I said something out of place? I thought you knew. Someone noticed your mother's name in the newspaper, and Mr Woods was despatched to see if it was the same Deirdre Briscoe Mr Pollard was looking for. Mr Woods brought back the photograph of your mother – didn't you know? Your father saw it, and that was enough. Also, the handkerchief with your blood on it has been sent away for analysis."

"The blood on my—" Peter stopped, suddenly realising why Mr Woods had been so anxious to give him a clean handkerchief that evening. He smiled to himself at the irony. *Joe's* blood was being tested for DNA to see if Mr Pollard was his father!

"Mr Pollard naturally wants proof that you are his son," Havis went on, unaware of Peter's internal celebration. "I don't think he'd be happy to give you his millions if you weren't, sir."

"No, I don't suppose he would," said Peter, his mind already working hard. "How long would it take for them to do the test?" he added, casually.

"Mr Pollard is expecting the blood and DNA results later today. Is there anything else you would like to ask, sir?"

"Not at the moment, thanks."

"I don't think your father will be much longer."

Even as he spoke, there was a squawk from his pocket, and Havis drew out a walkie-talkie. He said, "Yes, sir," into it, then looked up.

"He's ready now, Mr Peter."

Peter followed Havis like a dinghy behind the QE2, bobbing up and down in his wake. As he rushed along, he wondered what Mr Pollard – his "father" – would be like.

Havis knocked respectfully on a heavy door, then went in without waiting for a reply. He stood for a moment blocking Peter's view.

"Master Peter Briscoe, sir," he announced, then stood aside.

Peter walked into the room.

95

CHAPTER TEN

The Meeting

Mr Pollard was standing up to greet him, a figure in white shirt and trousers silhouetted against the dark oak panelling that lined the office. He looked younger than Peter had expected, except for the creases on his face and the weathered skin. He had blond, curly hair and blue eyes, and he seemed friendly enough. Peter approached the huge oak desk.

"Hello, Peter." Mr Pollard's voice was rough, like a wood-saw. He extended a hand, and Peter shook it. Havis withdrew.

Mr Pollard stared into Peter's face, hoping to see a likeness of himself. Peter's straight black hair and brown eyes stared unhelpfully back.

"You don't look anything like me," Mr Pollard said.

"No," said Peter. He was thinking, *it's hardly surprising if you're not my father*, but didn't dare to say it. There was information he wanted for himself, first.

"Well, sit down, then. Wha'd'ya fancy to drink? Whisky? Gin?" Mr Pollard laughed.

Peter wasn't in the mood for laughing. Instead, he was conscious of a strange feeling of something false in the room. Something bad.

"Just a lemonade, please," he said.

Mr Pollard pressed a button on his desk and Havis reappeared.

"A lemonade for Master Peter, please, Havis."

"Yes, sir."

Havis disappeared and Mr Pollard looked long and hard at

Peter again.

"It's taken me nearly thirteen years to find you," he said, at last. "I'm sorry if I stare a bit, but I can't believe you're here after all this time."

"That's all right."

"You don't seem very excited about seeing me."

Peter didn't smile.

"I always thought you were dead," he said solemnly.

Mr Pollard seemed slightly shocked.

"Who told you that?"

"Mum, of course."

"That wasn't right, was it?"

"No, I suppose not."

"Weren't you curious, Peter?"

"Only when Mum died."

"That's how I found you."

"Yes, I know."

"How did you know?"

"My uncle put Mum's maiden name in the newspapers when she died. Deirdre Briscoe."

"Ah, yes."

"But everyone knew her as Mrs Turner."

"What happened to Mr Turner?"

Peter paused, deciding not to tell Mr Pollard anything very helpful.

"He died when I was two," he lied, not flinching.

Mr Pollard's voice took on a sympathetic tinge, but still with the rough, grating edge.

"I see. Most unfortunate."

Peter looked down at his feet.

"Yes."

"You're obviously a bright lad, Peter, and the least I can do is to tell you my side of the story. I want to tell you so you understand and don't think badly of your long-lost dad. Fair enough?"

97

The door opened and Havis appeared with Peter's lemonade. He placed it on the desk, winked surreptitiously at Peter, and withdrew. Peter took a long draught.

A distant look came into Mr Pollard's eyes as he leaned back on his swivel chair. "Your mother and I lived together for a year," he began. "At the end, for some stupid reason, we quarrelled, and as far as your mum was concerned, it was the end. She walked out, didn't want to see me ever again. I pleaded with her to stay, but she wouldn't. I really loved Deirdre, and I tried to find her again . . ."

Peter took another sip of lemonade.

" . . .but I couldn't. I almost caught up with her once, but by the time I got there, she'd moved on. When you were due to be born, I still hadn't found her. I checked with the hospital, but there was nothing there. Eventually I checked up and saw a copy of your birth certificate. So at least I knew your name and when you were born."

Pity you didn't look for a death certificate, thought Peter, callously, surprised at himself for not caring. He took another sip of lemonade and carried on listening. It was funny to think that he already knew more than Mr Pollard did. Yet here he was, listening to Mr Pollard, when all the time Mr Pollard should have been listening to him.

"I searched the local telephone directory, scanned the voters lists, but I couldn't find Deirdre."

"Is that how you find missing people?" Peter interrupted, suddenly interested. "With a voters list?"

"It's one of the ways. My—"

"Where do you find the voters list?" he interrupted again.

"Local council. Why do you ask?"

"I'm just interested," said Peter, stone-faced, but thinking that he might find the information useful for himself.

"Well – my business was beginning to take off and I had contacts all over the country. When people owed me a favour I asked them to keep an eye out for Deirdre Briscoe in their local papers and voting lists. Then, a week ago, nearly thirteen years later, an old friend told me he'd seen the name in the deaths column in a London newspaper. *Deirdre Briscoe*. It was already four weeks old, but he spotted it when he was using it to light a bonfire. It was nearly a hundred miles away from Chichester, where we used to live, but I had to find out if it was the same person."

"So you sent Mr Woods," said Peter, accusingly. "And he pretended to be friendly with my uncle, and when my uncle invited him to the house he pinched the picture of my mother off the shelf in the sitting-room."

Mr Pollard stiffened, unprepared for the sudden outburst from his new-found son.

"Well, yes, Peter – but I had to find out if she was *my* Deirdre Briscoe, didn't I? How else could I know without seeing a picture? And as she called herself Mrs Caroline Turner, I needed to know if there was a Mr Turner looking after you, as well."

Peter said nothing. He hadn't smiled throughout the whole meeting, and Mr Pollard was beginning to notice.

"Does your uncle know *any* of this?" Mr Pollard went on.

"No."

"So how is it *you* know so much about it?"

Peter shrugged, afraid to give too much away.

"I just worked it out," he said. "That's all."

Suddenly, Mr Pollard banged the desk and laughed, a loud, coarse laugh.

"That's my boy!" he shouted. "That's my intelligent young lad! You'll be working in Daddy's firm in no time at this rate!"

Peter didn't tell him that he wouldn't work in his firm in a million years, but realised with a jolt that the worst of the inquisition was over. He felt a gentle smile of relief spreading across his face. Mr Pollard's laughter died away as he mistook Peter's smile for approval, and looked at him with a fatherly twinkle in his eye.

"Well?" he said.

Peter remembered to stay on his guard.

"Well, what?"

"What d'you think?"

"I don't know what you mean."

Mr Pollard searched the walls and ceiling for help.

"I've found you, Peter. *You're my son.* It's not *my* fault I haven't been in touch since the day you were born. It was your mother's fault."

"My mum was brilliant," said Peter coldly, "so don't you say anything against her." He felt the lump rising in his throat, and the tightening between his eyes.

"I'm sorry, Peter, I didn't mean it like that. I just want to make it up to you, but you'll have to help. It's a two-way thing."

Peter said nothing, still feeling hurt.

"If you come here to visit me, any time, you can have anything you want, Peter, I mean it. Anything you want at all. I'm not short of money, and I want to show you what it'll be like if you come and live with me. If you want your own camcorder, a go-kart, a boat, anything at all, just say."

The telephone rang.

Mr Pollard picked it up.

"Okay. I'll come down." He replaced the receiver and said to Peter, "You just make yourself comfortable, and I'll be back in ten minutes. Enjoy your lemonade."

"Okay."

The door closed and Peter was left on his own. He looked round. The sun was high over the nearby hills, bathing the room with a yellow glow. It shone on stacks of electronic equipment, computers and telephones, and other things Peter couldn't put a name to. And it shone on something he couldn't see in the far corner of the room. It was making a moving, circular reflection on the wall.

He stood up and went over to see what it was. It was on another desk in the corner, partly hidden by piles of books. It was a big tape, and it was turning on a big tape recorder. Peter wondered what it was doing. He pressed the stop button, rewound the tape several metres, then pressed "Play". Mr Pollard's voice came out of the speaker, loud and clear:

"If you come here to visit me, any time, you can have anything you want, Peter, I mean it. Anything you want at all. I'm not short of money, and I want to show you what it'll be like if you come and live with me. If you want your own camcorder, a go-kart, a boat, anything at all, just say."

On the tape he heard the sound of the telephone ringing and Mr Pollard's voice again:

"Okay. I'll come down."

Peter's hand was shaking now. Mr Pollard had recorded everything they'd said! He pressed "Record" and "Play" together to start it again so that Mr Pollard wouldn't notice he'd touched it. He glanced round nervously. There was another tape recorder next to it. Not turning. Not recording. Peter pressed "Rewind" on that one, then the "Play" button. Havis's voice came in mid-sentence:

" . . .have I said something out of place? I thought you knew. Someone noticed your mother's name in the newspaper, and Mr Woods was despatched to see if it was the same Deirdre Briscoe Mr Pollard was looking for. Mr Woods brought back the photograph of your mother – didn't you know? Your father saw it, and that was enough. Also, the handkerchief with your blood on it has been sent away for analysis."

Then came Peter's own voice:

"The blood on my—"

Then Havis's again:

"Mr Pollard naturally wants proof . . ."

Peter, alarmed, shut it off. The room he and Joe had been

in was bugged! Everything he had said to Havis, and to Joe, and everything Havis had said to them, had been recorded in Mr Pollard's office! He felt so grateful to Joe, remembering with horror Joe's warning message on the computer screen. He breathed a big sigh of relief. Good old Joe.

He tried not to panic, but did the only thing he could think of to destroy anything they might have said out of place. He rewound the tape to the beginning and pressed "Record" and "Play" on that one as well. The tape started turning.

Why would Mr Pollard want to listen to them?

Peter went back to his seat and tried to behave normally. Inside, his head was spinning. His premonition of evil hadn't been misplaced. Mr Pollard wanted something else, some secret, and Peter didn't know what. He recalled the words of his mother's letter. *"It breaks my heart to tell you that I've left you with a secret . . ."* He wondered if it was the same secret that Mr Pollard was after.

He sat in silence for another five minutes, wondering what he could possibly know that Mr Pollard wanted to find out.

Then Mr Pollard came back.

"Sorry, Peter," he said, sitting down. "I'm afraid I get these business interruptions all the time. Now – where were we?"

"You were saying I could have anything I want if I visit you," said Peter, straight-faced again.

Mr Pollard laughed.

"Is there something you want, then?"

"Not at the moment, thank you."

Mr Pollard's eyes settled on Peter in a friendly smile.

"Well, Peter. Now that I've made a little promise to you, I want you to do a little something for me."

Peter's defences immediately sprang to red alert. It had all been casual and friendly so far, but now a red light was flashing high up in his brain and his senses were sharpened for whatever else was to come. He looked his host straight in the eyes.

"You said I could have whatever I wanted," he said. "You didn't say I had to do anything for it."

Mr Pollard chuckled again.

"I like your spirit, son!" he said, and took a deep breath. "All I want from you is a bit of information, that's all."

"What about?"

"Well, first – did your mother leave you anything when she died?"

"Leave me anything?"

"The house?"

Peter couldn't see any harm in the question.

"No, she left the house to my uncle – but he has to look after me."

"What about money? Did she leave you any money?"

Peter's suspicions were still escalating. Why did Mr Pollard want to know about money if he was already a millionaire?

"No. She didn't leave any money. She didn't have any. The house was paid for when she died."

"Life assurance?"

"I think so. I think it was -" he plucked the word from his uncle's conversation with the insurance man – "in trust, or something."

"Ah, yes. And what about papers? Did she leave any papers?"

Peter was feeling more uncomfortable by the second.

"What sort of papers?"

Mr Pollard was watching him closely.

"Well – did she leave *any* papers?"

Peter's mind flew back to the box they'd found in the attic – the one he'd taken round to Joe's. What had Joe found in it that was so important – and so dangerous? Was it these "papers"?

"No," he lied. "Only her personal things. Just certificates

and things like that. Why?"

"No – other – papers?"

Peter reached for the comfort of his lemonade glass, but it was empty.

"I don't know what sort of papers you mean . . ."

"Well, if there weren't any other papers, there weren't any other papers, were there?"

Peter looked at Mr Pollard quizzically but didn't say anything. His host explained further.

"It's just that your mother had something that belonged to me, Peter. It was very important, and I just want it back, that's all."

"It can't be very important if you've done without it for thirteen years," said Peter, logically.

Mr Pollard laughed again and slapped the desk.

"You're not stupid, Peter, are you? I think you and I might get on very well together . . ."

Peter allowed him another weak grin.

"Well, let's leave it like this," said Mr Pollard. "If you ever find any papers that belonged to your mother – any at all – you let me have a look at them – okay? And I'll look after you – all right?"

"Why don't you just tell me what the papers are?" said Peter, simply. "Then I might be able to help."

"Oh, they were just papers – just business papers, that's all. A letter. A sort of contract."

"Okay," Peter promised, but he knew it wouldn't count as a promise, because he had his fingers crossed behind his back.

More than ever now, he wanted to get five minutes alone with Joe. He wanted to find out if it was the missing papers that Joe had found in the box.

CHAPTER ELEVEN

Fly Away, Peter

As soon as he was back with Joe, and Havis had gone,
Peter's fingers flew over the keyboard, and Joe read the new
message:
"THIS ROOM IS BUGGED.   TAPE   RECORDER   IN
POLLARD'S ROOM."
Joe nodded and Peter backspaced the message off the
screen.   Their eyes met in deeper understanding of the
danger they were in, although Peter was aware he knew less
than Joe about the details.
Peter thought about the tape recordings. Why would Mr
Pollard want to monitor them so closely? It seemed that
there was something more important about his mother and
his past than just him, Peter Briscoe. Mr Pollard's interest in
him as a son had seemed quite genuine – but underneath
there lurked the missing papers.
Was that what Joe had found in the dusty box? It was
becoming seriously urgent to get Joe alone for five minutes
and find out what was going on.
Peter didn't see Mr Pollard again that day. Lunch was
brought to their room by Havis, who explained that Mr
Pollard had another urgent business matter to attend to.
After they'd eaten, Joe went to find a bathroom, and Peter
lazed on the four-poster bed. He could see the sky, pale blue
with a few wispy clouds. It was much quieter than at home.
There was no traffic noise at all, just an occasional airliner at
high altitude grating its way across the heavens.
For just a few minutes, the house grew silent. No one
came or went along corridors, there was no sound of music

or muffled conversation, not even the chiming of a clock. There was the single squeak of a door somewhere, or a floorboard, then no more.

When the voice came calling, it was almost as though he was expecting it. It was clearer than it had ever been before. Not unbearably loud, or shouting loud, but just easier to hear. He still didn't know what it said. It sounded as if it was calling him by name, yet it wasn't him, or it wasn't his name. He concentrated his mind again, trying to call back. He didn't know what to say, so just repeated "Hello" in his mind over and over again. The voice stayed with him for only thirty seconds, but for the first time *it seemed to have direction*. Peter started turning his head slowly, trying to find where it was coming from, but as soon as he made the move, the voice was gone.

Then Joe came back.

"Do you fancy a stroll in those woods down there," he said, pointing, "before we go back home?" Then, half joking, "I fancy some exercise after lazing around in a Rolls all morning."

Peter had never seen such a massive grin on his friend's face as Joe said it. Havis gave the okay, and ten minutes later they had found a patch of woodland with good trees in it where they could see if anyone approached. They climbed to the middle of one and sat in the fork.

"No one'll hear us up here," said Joe.

"What's going on, then?" said Peter, instinctively talking in a whisper as a double safety measure. "What have you found?"

Joe untucked his shirt and pulled out a long brown envelope from the belt of his jeans.

Peter stared as Joe lowered his voice still further.

"Before you look at this," said Joe, waving the envelope, "I'll give you a choice. *Do you want to carry on being a millionaire's son for the rest of your life, or do you want to look at it now?"*

"I don't know what you're talking about," groaned Peter.

"Put it this way. If you look at this now, you'll want to go away – now . . ."

"Go where – ? What do you mean, Joe? Why have you started talking in *riddles*? Why don't you say what you *mean*?"

"If you *don't* look at it – if you let me burn it – you can still be a millionaire – that's all. Otherwise . . ."

Peter looked at the papers as if they were an opponent's cards in a game of poker.

"What are they? Where did you get them? Not in the box. We looked in the box."

Joe felt his patience being pushed beyond reasonable endurance.

"Yes, from the box, superbrain!" he hissed.

"Let me see!"

Joe held the newspaper out of reach.

"So you don't want to carry on being a millionaire?"

"No – it's boring. I'd rather see the papers."

"Okay, then, I warned you. You'd better see this one first."

Suddenly, Peter felt a chill groping down his back that wasn't just the autumn wind. Joe glanced around to make sure that no one had crept up on them in the last few minutes, then pulled a newspaper cutting from the envelope.

"*I cut this from the newspaper that was lining the box,*" he said. "I went through everything else three times, and the newspaper was the only thing I hadn't looked at. I started reading it when I noticed this. Look. *It's ringed with red crayon.* That *must* mean it's important."

Joe pointed to the corner of the small rectangle where it had been chewed away by the mouse that had eaten the box. Peter squinted in the dull light in the tree and tried to read it:

" . . . *Baby* . . . *tched* . . . *tside* . . *rocer's*," ran what was left

107

of the headline.

"Young Baby Snatched Outside Grocer's?" said Joe, helping. Peter read on:

"*. . . baby boy, just one . . . old, was taken from . . . am outside Prince's . . . ers in Chichester on . . . nday afternoon. . . . e baby, James Michael . . arwood, disappeared while his mother, Mrs Janice Harwood, had gone into the shop 'for just a few items'. No witnesses to the incident have come forward, and James's parents are distraught and heart-broken. They have another son, aged 3, who was at playschool when the abduction took place. Police are appealing for witnesses who might have seen anyone acting suspiciously in that area on Monday afternoon to come forward. They have also asked if anyone knows of a person who might have acquired a baby without any apparent pregnancy, or of any mother who might have lost her baby recently.*"

"My God!" said Peter, stunned. "Is that me? Snatched from a pram?!" At last he realised the shocking truth of his mother's secret – the secret she could never tell him.

"It must be you, mustn't it?" said Joe. "Why would she put red crayon round it if it wasn't? *She wanted you to find it*, that's why she left it there. I was dying to tell you, but I couldn't take any chances—"

"You're right, Joe. I can't stay here – not now." Peter held the little rectangle firmly. "What are the other things you've got?"

Joe handed him the long brown envelope.

"This envelope fell out of the newspaper. She'd tucked it inside."

Peter fondled it, trying to guess its contents like the birthday present they'd tried to find. The address on the front was to Frank Pollard at an address in Chichester. The postmark was dated three months before Peter was born.

"Those are the papers Mr Pollard wants," said Joe. "I tell you, they're dynamite!"

"*Then I'll have them here, young man!*" snapped a voice nearby.

The two boys' heads spun round. A man in a dark coat was standing in the shadow of the trees a few metres below them. They saw his nearly-bald head, his chubby figure, his moustache, his glasses.

"Mr Woods!" shouted Peter.

Joe was the first to realise their mistake. They hadn't checked their surroundings again, and their voices had gradually crept above a whisper. Mr Woods, well practised as a private eye, had sneaked up on them and overheard the last few words – the words he'd been waiting to hear for many years.

But Mr Woods had made a mistake as well. He should have kept quiet and grabbed the boys as they came down, but in his own excitement he had given himself away.

Peter saw his chubby hand reach into his pocket, and just caught the glint of silver moving upwards in the shadows. For one horrible, frightening moment, he thought it was a gun.

Instead, the silver object went to Mr Woods' lips. He

blew. A shrill whistle cut through the night air, once, twice, three times, and sent a shiver of horror through Peter and Joe.

Peter froze, but Joe was galvanised into action. He grabbed the papers from Peter, pushed the newspaper clipping into the envelope, then shoved the whole package back into Peter's grasp.

"Take those!" he hissed in Peter's ear. "When I jump, run! Get away from here fast, before the others come!"

Peter had no time to think much, or say anything. Joe leapt from the tree and landed with both feet on Mr Woods' chest. The private detective went down like a sack of turnips and lay groaning, trying to get his breath.

Peter jumped past them and started running, leaping along the path through the trees and away from the house. There was no sign of Joe, so Peter ran back. By this time, Joe was squirming on the ground next to Mr Woods, shouting "Let go of me!" and trying to kick him, and Mr Woods was holding on to Joe with one hand like a monkey to a banana, blowing his whistle with the other. Peter stood, undecided. Joe saw him.

"Get away, you idiot!" he screamed. "Go! Quick!"

"Where?" panted Peter.

"Just go, you idiot! Don't you read the *newspapers*?"

Peter looked down at the envelope clutched in his fingers, and suddenly realised what Joe meant. Without waiting a second longer, he ran off through the trees.

As he ran, he realised that the earth-shattering change had taken place. *He wasn't Peter Briscoe any more.* He was James Michael Harwood, and he was on his way home to Chichester after thirteen long years.

CHAPTER TWELVE

Hunted

Peter slid the envelope into his pocket and ran as fast as he could through the trees. Bony hands of branches filled the half darkness ahead, clutching at his clothes and whipping his face as he pounded his way to the edge of the wood. He emerged from the trees after fifty or sixty metres and found the first obstacle lurking in his path – a barbed wire fence. He ducked between the top two strands and flew on, down a sloping field towards a hedge and a country lane. The hedge was too thick to get through. He ran along it to the right, found a small hole and squeezed through. Checking for cars both ways, he crossed the lane, then followed it to the right until he found a five-bar gate. He climbed into the field, then stopped for breath, out of sight of the road.

Dark clouds were sliding across the sky. Peter stood in the rapidly fading light, heart thumping, trying to get his bearings. He decided to make for the village and a telephone. He hadn't noticed in the Rolls Royce which way Norman had taken them. He'd been in a dream the whole time. He felt that the village lay to the right, and he set off across the field. Sheep scattered as he ran.

A few moments later he heard a vehicle. A car sped past, very fast, travelling to where he thought the village lay. It could have been anyone, but it might have been Mr Pollard. Frightened of being seen in daylight, dull as it was, he crawled into a dark copse and lay there until the light started to fade from the sky altogether. It took over two hours, but he still felt safer that way. When it seemed gloomy enough, he crawled out.

111

It was already darker than he'd realised. After two more fields, Peter began to get worried. He could see virtually nothing. He was afraid of running into a barbed wire fence – or, worse, a bull. Apart from that, he only had on a jumper and jeans, and he knew if he stopped again he would soon get cold. He had to find safe shelter, and he had to find it quickly. There was a single light in the distance ahead, perhaps a mile away. He decided to head for it in a straight line, and started to run again.

A hedge loomed up and he lost sight of the light. He reached the hedge and ran along it to the right. No way round. He ran as far as he could to the left and found the same thing. He would have to get through it, somehow. He felt carefully with his hands to make sure it wasn't prickly, then lay flat on the cold grass and started to force his way forward. He made his way over a thick piece of trunk and came full stop against another, higher up. He couldn't get between them. He wriggled out, went a few metres further on, tried again. No good. The third time he was lucky. With a quiet groan of triumph, he squirmed through into the field.

The light of the house was visible again and he ran on, slowing down as he approached a thin line of trees. Probably a ditch, and possibly a barbed wire fence. He crept forward. It was both. He stooped carefully between the wicked strands, felt his way carefully down the ditch, then across it to the edge of a ploughed field. He went round its left edge, across another ditch and through two more fences. At last he was in a meadow next to the house, the lights shining yellow. He crept from side to side, trying to see if there was shelter. At the top of the drive, looking abandoned, was an old car. He tried the door. It was unlocked, and he climbed in.

Peter was still warm from running, but he knew he wouldn't stay warm for long. He lay back on the cold seat, taking stock of his situation. He had no money at all. The envelope was in one pocket and in the other was a dirty handkerchief. More than anything, he wanted to read the letter that Joe had found. He wanted to see what it said, but there wasn't enough light inside the car. Whatever it said, it was obviously wanted badly by Mr Pollard. It had to be important if he was still looking for it after thirteen years.

Suddenly, Peter wondered which of them Mr Pollard had wanted to find most – the letter, or his son? He felt glad he wasn't Mr Pollard's son. He wouldn't want a father who was more interested in a piece of paper than his own child. It was sad that the real Peter had died when he was one day old. The poor kid hadn't had a chance.

A shiver ran through him as the night air started to grope its way through his thin sweater. At least he was out of the wind. He tried to relax and think ahead. If he was caught, Mr Pollard would get the letter. Joe hadn't said it in so many words, but he knew what Joe meant: it must never get into Mr Pollard's hands. So Peter had only two choices: he could hide the letter, or he could make sure he didn't get caught.

He decided not to get caught.

If he waited until morning, he would be travelling in daylight. Mr Pollard's men would be out looking for him, in cars and on foot, and that would be dangerous. It would be better to travel by night. He could rest during the day, when it was warmer – and safer.

He would wait another hour for the immediate search to be abandoned. When the hour was up, he would follow the drive out on to the road. Then he'd be able to run fast, without hitting barbed wire or bulls. In the meantime he would have a little sleep . . .

He wondered if Joe would have the sense to phone his parents and make up some excuse about not being home. He hoped they would phone his uncle Len as well . . .

He curled up in a ball in a corner of the seat. As sleep came creeping up on him, he could hear the voice fluttering against the windows of his mind, like a hapless moth striving for the light. As it faded, he slept.

Joe continued to struggle and curse and kick, but couldn't free himself from the enemy. The more he tried to pull away, the more Mr Woods' grip tightened on his wrist, like a bat hanging on to a branch. Annoyingly, he kept blowing his whistle right next to Joe's ear.

Within minutes two more men appeared and Joe was dragged back to the house. He was taken straight to Mr Pollard's room, but they kept him waiting outside while Mr Woods went in to tell his side of the story. When Mr Woods reappeared, Joe was led inside.

His first sight of the legendary Mr Pollard did not give the impression of a happy man. The face stared at Joe balefully across its desk as its hand picked up the telephone.

"No calls," said a grating, impatient voice. Mr Pollard slammed the receiver down, then spoke to Joe. "Where is Peter?" he demanded.

"He ran away," said Joe.

"I know he ran away," said Mr Pollard, irritably. "Mr Woods told me. But you know where he's gone."

"No I don't."

"You gave him something."

"No I didn't."

"You said 'Take those'. What were 'those'?"

"Aspirins," said Joe, calmly. "He had a headache."

"Why did he run off, then?"

"Mr Woods frightened him. We were just walking in the woods, chatting, when that ton of concrete" – he indicated Mr Woods – "jumped out of a tree and flattened me for no reason. It's no wonder Peter ran off."

"Can you believe that!" spluttered Mr Woods, interrupting.

Joe ploughed on.

"By the time I got any breath back, Mr Woods had my wrist and wouldn't let go, so I started kicking him."

"That's hardly true!" said Mr Woods, interrupting for the second time. "I followed them. They climbed a tree and I sneaked up on them. I had to get close to hear what they were up to, and when I was close enough this one said" – he cocked a thumb in Joe's direction – "and I quote: '*Those are the papers Mr Pollard wants. I tell you, they're dynamite!*' I said 'I'll have them here, then', and this one jumped on *me*, and your son ran off."

"So who's got the papers?" said Mr Pollard. His face was dark with suppressed anger.

"Don't know what you're talking about," said Joe. "Mr Woods is making it all up as he goes along. It was *him* who jumped on *us*. No wonder Peter ran off."

With a great effort on Mr Pollard's part, his anger slowly evaporated. He changed the subject.

"Tell me something else," he said. "Do you know when Peter's birthday is?"

Joe couldn't see any harm in the question, and was lured into answering.

"It's on Friday. The twenty-fifth of October. There's still time to buy him a present."

Mr Pollard ignored the sarcasm.

"Did you know his mother?"

Now Joe understood where the questions were leading.

"Yes. Why?"

"What was her name?"

"Mrs Turner."

"Did you know *Mr* Turner?"

"No."

"Do you know what her name was before she married?"

"Briscoe, of course. The same as Peter. Deirdre Briscoe."

Mr Pollard stared, motionless, his voice cold as ice.

115

"How did you know that?"

Joe shrugged.

"Stands to reason, doesn't it," he said cheerfully, "if Peter's name was Briscoe?"

"Mmmm." Mr Pollard, deflated, stood up and started pacing behind his desk, side to side. "You see, Joe, there's something really odd going on, and I can't understand it. I think you might be able to help." He stopped pacing, opened a drawer in his desk, and pulled out a dirty, bloodstained handkerchief. Half of it was missing. Joe sensed something familiar about it. It was probably the one he'd seen Mr Woods putting into a plastic bag in his car. It was probably the one that Peter had used to bandage Joe's finger when he had fallen over in Peter's hallway.

"This is Peter's handkerchief, Joe, but I wouldn't expect you to know that. One dirty handkerchief is much like another, really, isn't it?"

"I suppose so," said Joe.

"But this one's got blood on it. Peter's blood."

"Poor Peter."

"Yes. Poor Peter, as you say. I had the blood analysed by a friend of mine at a university – for the blood group and the DNA fingerprint. I've just had the results on the fax."

Mr Woods leaned forward perceptibly, anxious to hear the result of the test that he himself had suggested.

"So?" said Joe, trying to look uninterested.

"The blood group doesn't match mine," said Mr Pollard slowly. "But that isn't conclusive. What *is* conclusive is this: *the DNA doesn't match with mine.*"

"So?" said Joe again.

"That means *Peter can't be my son*, doesn't it?"

Before answering, Joe thought of the consequences of the conversation. Peter would be much safer if Mr Pollard continued to believe that Peter was his own son.

"It doesn't mean that at all," he said, calmly.

116

Mr Pollard tilted his head.

"What?"

Joe repeated himself.

"I said, it doesn't mean that at all."

Mr Pollard looked at Joe long and hard, trying to see if he was just thick, or plain stupid.

"*If the DNA doesn't match, he can't be my son,*" he repeated, shaking his head slowly from side to side. His voice was heavy with sarcasm. He mouthed the words clearly, so even the thick oak desk could understand. "Don't they teach you science and biology at school these days?"

"Yes, they do," said Joe, still calm. "That's how I know."

Mr Pollard looked exasperated.

"Well how do you make out that he's my son, then, if the DNA doesn't match?"

"Simple," said Joe. He gave Mr Pollard an unwavering stare. "*Because it's my blood on the handkerchief.*"

There was a stunned silence. Before either man could speak, Joe held out his hand and displayed the almost-healed scab on the side of his little finger.

"I fell down in Peter's hall and cut it," he explained. "Peter lent me his handkerchief."

Mr Woods' eyes flicked from Joe to Mr Pollard and back again, twice.

"He's lying," he said. "All kids have a cut somewhere."

Joe gave him a withering look.

"My blood group is A rhesus D positive," he said, simply.

"How do you know something like that," challenged Mr Woods. "I don't know mine."

"Try asking your doctor," said Joe.

A wave of emotion passed over Mr Pollard's face, and he sat down heavily. There was relief on his face, not anger.

"That's right," he said. "That's the group that came up on the test. A rhesus D positive."

"Told you," said Joe, rubbing it in.

"I *knew* he was my son," crackled Mr Pollard. He slapped the desk and laughed. Then he looked at Joe again, suddenly serious. "So that just leaves the papers, doesn't it?"

"I told you," said Joe, "I don't know what you're talking about." He looked Mr Pollard straight in the eyes. "And I'd like to go home now, please."

Mr Pollard turned to Mr Woods and snapped out a set of instructions.

"We'll have to find Peter," he said. "He won't have gone far. Get all the cars patrolling the roads between here and the village. He's bound to make for there. It's obvious. Stay out all night if necessary, and all tomorrow. At first light get the helicopter up. And have someone watching every telephone box in the village."

"There's only one," said Mr Woods, starting for the door. He settled a sinister look on to Joe. "I'll watch that one personally."

Mr Pollard turned to Joe with a supercilious stare.

"See?" he said. "Peter won't get far."

Soon, Joe heard the sound of cars leaving the drive at high speed.

"Next, I want you to telephone your parents," said Mr Pollard, "and tell them you've been delayed. Tell them the car has broken down. Tell them you'll be back in the morning. And make sure they tell Peter's uncle, too. There's no sense in causing undue worry, is there?"

Joe tried to work out whether he should co-operate or not. If he refused to telephone, they would both be reported missing, and the police would be involved. If he told his mother that Peter had escaped and was making his way to Chichester, she would panic, probably via hysterics. Especially if she knew he was carrying damning evidence and being chased cross-country by a gaggle of greasy gangsters. The police would be involved immediately, then, and Peter's journey of discovery would become impossible.

118

On the other hand, if he told her that all was well, and really sorry for not letting her know he was going with Peter, and that they'd be home in the morning, she'd probably be all right – for twenty-four hours at least. And twenty-four hours was what Peter needed more than anything.

He picked up the telephone.

"Mum?"

"Joe? Where are you? I've been so worried."

"Why? I went out with Peter, that's all. To see his . . . uncle. But his uncle's car's broken down and we can't get back."

"That doesn't matter. As long as you're safe."

"Can you tell his Uncle Len?"

"Yes, Joe. It's such a relief you weren't at Peter's house today."

"Why?"

"I'm so glad you weren't there," wailed Mrs Robson. "Anything might have happened. It's been ransacked."

Joe stiffened.

"*Ransacked*? Was anything taken?"

"No, nothing at all. But they turned the place inside out."

Joe glanced across at Mr Pollard, who stood stony-faced as Mrs Robson continued.

"It was as if they were looking for something *in particular . . .*"

It was the cold that woke Peter up – and the daylight streaming in through the car windows, shining on his eyelids. In the same instant he realised he had overslept and that his plan to travel at night had already gone wrong. He looked at his watch. Ten minutes to seven.

Would they be out searching for him so early?

He decided not to wait. Carefully, he opened the door of the car and stepped on to the drive. Another car was parked nearer the house. He hurried past it and out on to the road, hoping that no one had seen him from the house windows. He started running. The countryside was very open, with few trees, deep ditches, and neat hedges with narrow tops and wide bases. Three times he heard a car in the distance and hid in the ditch until it passed. It was the same car each time, going up and down the same road.

At the first road junction there was a sign pointing left to the village. Opposite was a sign for a public footpath with "Little Haston 2 miles" written on it. Peter heard the car again in the distance and decided to get off the road and on to the footpath. If he ran at a steady pace, he'd be in the village in about half an hour.

He'd only been going for five minutes when he heard the chop-chop of a helicopter in the distance. He watched from behind a hedge until he saw it, sweeping low over the countryside. It was Mr Pollard's helicopter. Without a second to spare, he crept along at the base of the hedgerow until he was under a tree, then climbed a little way up it where he couldn't be seen from the air. The helicopter lumbered across the sky, twisting this way and that, then turned and swept across at a different angle.

As soon as it had passed to the other side of the hedgerow, Peter ran as fast as he could to the next tree, and hid again. Once more the helicopter turned, then went off in a new direction altogether, until the thump-thump of air was just a distant blur of sound.

Peter ran and ran, now choosing routes that were in trees where possible, or skirting round fields next to hedges rather than going straight across the middle. But every time he diverted he made sure he came back to the footpath further on.

As he approached another road he heard a car coming, and took cover. The same one passed a few minutes later, going back the other way. Whatever else Peter thought, he knew that Mr Pollard and his men intended finding him.

When the patrolling car had disappeared for the second time, he crossed the road ahead of him. Now he could see houses on the outskirts of the village. He slowed down. Would Mr Pollard have men posted to watch out for him? Of course he would.

Peter needed time to rest and think. There was a thick copse of trees away to his left. Listening out for helicopters and cars, he made for it at a run. It was a good place, and he found a hollow in some overgrown bushes where he could hide. Without waiting to get his breath back he pulled the envelope from his pocket and examined its contents. Apart from the newspaper cutting, which he carefully replaced, he found the letter that Mr Pollard wanted so badly. With it was a coded message on a piece of paper.

CHAPTER THIRTEEN

The Letter

At the time when Peter took refuge in the copse, Joe was still in Mr Pollard's house, locked in the room where he had spent the night. He had already discovered that escape from the second floor was impossible without a ladder.

When Havis came in with breakfast, Joe tackled him.

"Did you know Peter's run away, Havis?"

"That has been brought to my attention, Mr Joe. Mr Pollard is doing everything he can to find him."

"Do you know why Mr Pollard's keeping me locked in?"

"No, sir. But I'm sure Mr Pollard has his reasons."

"But I want to go home now. My mum's worried enough as it is."

"Mr Pollard has forbidden it, I'm afraid."

"So I've been kidnapped, then?"

"I wouldn't say that, Mr Joe. Mr Pollard is worried that you might run after Peter, and then both of you would be lost. You are his responsibility, after all." As he spoke, Havis raised his eyebrows, held a finger to his lips and gestured towards the walls and ceiling.

It was obvious that Havis, too, knew the room was bugged. Was he giving Joe a sign that he was on their side? Joe was no fool, and he wasn't going to be tricked into telling Havis anything that he didn't want him to know.

"Oh," Joe said aloud. Then, reaching up to whisper in Havis's ear, he added, *"Do you know the real reason why Mr Pollard wants Peter?"*

Havis replied in a voice so hushed, Joe could hardly hear it.

"I don't know what you mean, Mr Joe?"

"Well," Joe whispered back, "I'll tell you the real reason if you promise not to tell Mr Pollard."

Havis looked at him meaningfully.

"I'd be most interested, Mr Joe." Then, reverting to his normal voice, he said, "I'll fetch your tray in twenty minutes, Mr Joe," and withdrew from the room, locking the door again.

Joe ate his breakfast with hopes slightly higher, but still calculating how much Havis could really be trusted. After all, he was one of Mr Pollard's men. On the other hand, Mr Pollard already knew Peter had the letter – he was bound to believe Mr Woods' version of the story. So telling Havis that Peter had it wouldn't exactly be giving anything away to the enemy.

Even if it did, no harm was likely to come to either of them, *but only as long as Mr Pollard kept on believing that Peter was his son.*

Peter made himself comfortable amongst the bushes and opened the envelope. He saw again that it was addressed to Frank Pollard at a house in Chichester, and dated three months before Peter Briscoe was born. It was written in scruffy handwriting:

Frank,
Here's your copy of the code showing where I've hidden the stuff. Keep it safe until it blows over. Someone may have welshed on me, so if I'm jugged, we'll have to square it when I get out. If they come for me, I'll burn my copy, so don't worry.
Reg.

Peter read it again, realising at last why it was something Mr Pollard was so anxious to get back. It was, possibly, the only surviving evidence that could link him to a past crime and put him behind bars.

He looked at the coded message:

```
TNQBM  HLVII  ENQLF  YUNEO  SLVMQ  RVKEG
TIVKG  BBPOQ  24793  3TXGT  YVVIZ  SSHFX
```

He knew it told where the "stuff" was hidden, and seemed to leave little doubt that the man who claimed to be his father was nothing less than a criminal – a big criminal who would do anything to get the letter back and keep his record clean.

Peter thought of his mother. She must have read the letter all those years ago, perhaps by mistake. Only then had she realised that her darling Frank was a criminal. That was why she'd run away from him – not because they'd quarrelled. And that was why Mr Pollard had wanted to find her so badly – as long as she had the letter and the coded key, Mr Pollard wasn't safe from justice. It was dangerous evidence against a clever man who had so far managed to avoid being caught.

Peter carefully folded them again, put them back in the envelope, and pushed it down his shirt into his belt. He stood up and looked around.

His next task was to get to a telephone. He had heard the helicopter several times since he'd been hiding, and he knew the village would be seething with Mr Pollard's men. At all costs, he had to stop them getting their greedy hands on the letter. He knew he'd be letting his mother down if he didn't.

When the sky was quiet, he scrambled out of his hiding place and ran across to where he thought the footpath lay. It wasn't marked. There were houses away to the left, mostly obscured by trees, and something that looked like a school. There were a few single trees dotted around, and a wooden shack with a corrugated roof to his right. On the horizon of the field ahead of him he could make out a low iron bridge with a wooden platform leading up to it. It was too far away to risk a run in the open. There were a few sparse bushes where a hedge had overgrown and thinned out, and further to the left a wide, watery ditch that might have been a river if it rained enough. It was closer to the school, but it was safer than running in the open. He ran towards the ditch, then picked up the faint line of a sheep track. He thought of running in the ditch, but it would be slower, and anyway his feet would get wet.

He reached the wooden platform safely, clambered through the side, then ran across the iron bridge, over a river. His footsteps sounded strangely hollow on the concrete. There was a house straight ahead with a disused water-wheel at the side. The path went right past the corner. He ran up through a meadow of long grass and emerged on a wide dusty bridleway.

He was almost in the heart of the village. He could see the square brick tower of a church sticking up through the treetops. There was a big sports field on his left, too exposed to run across. Instead, he veered left towards a row of tall poplar trees, across the lawn of a big white house, and through their shrubbery.

From there he crept towards the main road, hidden by fences, and cautiously put his head out. To the right was the open-limit sign leading out of the village. To the left was a shop. Next to that was the telephone box, and next to the telephone box was a light green sports car.

Peter retreated. One glimpse had confirmed the worst: the occupant of the sports car was Mr Woods, and he looked as if he was there to stay.

Peter went back the way he had come, and stood behind a tree to think.

What he wanted was a telephone – and most houses had telephones. All he needed to do was to knock on someone's door, say he was lost, and ask could he use their phone?

Filled with new energy, he decided to try the big white house. He tramped back through the shrubbery, across the lawn, and through the gate that led to the front. There was a Jaguar parked in the drive, and two smaller cars. He rang the bell. A fierce-looking woman came to the door.

"What do you want?"

"Please, Miss, I'm lost and I wondered if I could use your telephone?"

"Certainly not!" she said, and slammed the door.

Dispirited, Peter wandered back round the drive, his feet crunching on the gravel. As he passed the Jaguar, his eyes lit up. There was a telephone inside it. He looked back at the house. The woman was standing at the downstairs window, watching him. He wandered casually into the side road and turned left.

When he thought it was safe, he crept back towards the drive entrance again, stopping short to look through the hedge. The woman was no longer at the window. He slipped into the drive, crouching low, keeping the cars between himself and the house as much as possible. He reached the Jaguar and lay down on the gravel at the side away from the house windows. He waited thirty seconds to make sure no one had seen him. There was no sound. He reached his hand up and pressed the car's back door handle. There was a pleasing little thud as the door yielded. He inched it open and wriggled himself on to the back seat, still lying down, then pulled the door gently closed so it wouldn't be noticed from the house. He could see the upstairs windows, but that was all.

He took a deep breath. He reached his hand between the front seats and grabbed the mobile telephone. The owner hadn't switched it off, so it was satisfyingly ready for use.

Then he suddenly wondered – who was he going to call? It was no good trying to talk to Joe, because the lines into Passmeadow Hall were probably bugged, and he didn't know the number, anyway. It was no use phoning home because his uncle would already have left for work, unless he was talking to the police about Peter's disappearance. Apart from that, he wanted to go to Chichester, not back home. Even if he could remember his uncle's business number, his uncle would only make him go back. He didn't want to ring the police, either, because they'd just take him home as well. *He wanted to go to Chichester, and nothing else was good enough.*

He tried to think what Joe would do, and the very thought gave him the idea. He'd phone Joe's mother.

He lay down on the car seat, gazing at the upstairs window of the house, and punched in Joe's number.

"Hello?"

"Is that Mrs Robson?"

"Yes. Who's that? Is it Peter?"

"Yes."

"Hello, Peter. I'm so glad you're both safe. It was very naughty of you to go off like that without telling anyone. Now you've come unstuck, haven't you?"

Rather than feeling guilty, Peter was filled with a huge surge of relief. Joe must have telephoned already.

"I suppose so. I'm really sorry – but I wondered if you could do me a favour?"

"You don't sound very sorry. Go on, I'm listening."

"If Joe phones, can you just tell him I'm—" Peter rose up from the seat for inspiration and saw the church tower rising above the treetops – "tell him I'm in the churchyard."

"I thought he was with you?"

"Well, he is, but if he rings, just tell him—" Peter suddenly saw a face at the upstairs window of the house, and his speech accelerated – "I'm-in-the-churchyard-please-don't-forget-Bye!"

He slammed the telephone into its holder and tumbled out on to the drive as quickly as he could. The face that had spotted him using its car phone had already disappeared from the bedroom window and was on its way down.

Peter started to run, glancing back at the house as he went. The front door was already open, and a man big enough to blot out the sky was filling the drive with himself and some very bad language. He started after Peter at speed, shouting.

"Come back here, you! What d'you think you're doing!"

There were lots of worse words, but Peter didn't stay to learn them. He had no intention of coming back there, or of revealing what he thought he was doing. He moved up a gear and disappeared round the side of the house. He darted across the lawn and back into the shrubbery. The man gave up. Peter hurried on until he came to a footpath, then stopped to get his breath back.

The little footpath ran along the back of the churchyard. In one direction it led round to the main street, and in the other it joined up with the path by the sports field. In between the two, in the middle, was a white wooden gate leading into the churchyard itself. Peter opened it and went in.

To his right was an old wooden hut. He approached and tried the door, but it was padlocked. He looked through a gap and saw that it was full of gardening implements. He went behind it. Perfect. There was a line of tall hedges between the hut and the church, a large heap of grass cuttings on the right hand side, and the thick hedge that enclosed the churchyard behind and to the left.

He chose a patch of grass that couldn't be seen from anywhere, and lay down. He was hungry, and he was tired.

He closed his eyes and slept.

CHAPTER FOURTEEN

In the Churchyard

When Havis returned to collect Joe's tray, he pointed to the window, undid the lock and threw open the casement. For one horrible moment Joe thought he was going to be thrown two floors to his death. Instead, Havis leaned out of the window and gestured for Joe to sit beside him on the sill.

He whispered like a ghost in Joe's ear.

"The bug won't pick up our voices outside the window, Mr Joe," he said. His eyes narrowed, and Joe still didn't know whether the narrowed eyes were on his side, or Pollard's. "The windows downstairs are closed – we'll be safe here."

"How do I know I can trust you?" said Joe.

"I'm afraid you don't."

Joe had to take some chances. He had nothing to lose, and no other options. But he had to be careful.

"Do you know where Mr Pollard *really* gets all his money?" he said.

"I told you, Mr Joe. He buys and sells on the international market. He makes hundreds of international telephone calls, and has many foreign visitors."

"Well," said Joe, without wasting time, "he's a crook."

"I beg your pardon, sir?"

"He's a crook."

Havis looked grave, but interest flickered in his eyelids.

"It's very clever of you to reach such a drastic conclusion in twenty-four hours, Mr Joe."

"Peter's got a letter that proves it. That's why Mr Pollard's so keen to find him."

Havis looked at Joe quizzically.

"Surely he's only keen to find Mr Peter because he's his son?"

"Why doesn't he tell the police he's missing, then?" Joe challenged.

"He naturally doesn't want a fuss made in public, sir. '*Man finds lost son after thirteen years, and loses him again after five hours.*' As a newspaper story, it wouldn't make Mr Pollard look good."

"So why's he keeping *me* locked up?"

Havis was beginning to falter as Joe's arguments bombarded him one after another.

"He told me he was afraid you might run after Mr Peter and get lost as well. Then he would have double the worry. In the end, he has a responsibility to your parents, especially as you didn't tell them you were coming here."

"That's rubbish!" said Joe. "He knows Peter might give the police his precious piece of paper. Once the police have seen it, they'll start asking questions."

"I'm not fully convinced, Mr Joe."

Joe's voice hissed on at speed.

"Did you know Peter's house was *ransacked* yesterday?"

Havis was genuinely shocked.

"Surely not, sir!"

"Phone my mother. She'll tell you. Nothing was stolen, but they must have been looking for those papers."

Havis's face was serious.

"I'm sorry, sir, but I'm under strict instructions . . ."

"That's rubbish as well!" hissed Joe. He searched his brain for more inspiration. "I bet if I tell you what the letter says, you'll believe me!"

"Please do, sir." His eyes narrowed again, once more making Joe wonder how loyal he was to his employer.

Havis listened carefully as Joe related the story of the box from Peter's attic, but without mentioning the diary, the death certificate, or the newspaper report.

"That's what they were after when they searched the house yesterday," said Joe. Then he told Havis the contents of the letter.

At last, Havis had run out of things to say. He leaned hard against the window frame, analysing everything Joe had been telling him.

Joe whispered on.

"I know Mr Pollard has been looking for Peter for thirteen years . . ."

"It's been an obsession with Mr Pollard, sir."

" . . .but I think he wanted the letter more than he wanted Peter. *I bet that's why Peter's mother ran away.* I bet *she* read the letter and realised he was a crook. That's why she didn't want anything more to do with him. She ran away and changed her name and hid the letter in case she might need it, if Mr Pollard found her and started bothering her."

"It seems possible, Mr Joe . . ."

Havis was wavering, but not wavering enough. Joe decided to risk bringing out his trump card.

"If I show you something," he said, "will you promise, promise, promise never *never* to tell Mr Pollard until Peter's safe?"

"What do you mean by safe, Mr Joe?"

"Away from Mr Pollard for good."

"But Peter is his *son* . . ."

"That's just it," Joe lowered his voice even more. "He's not!" He reached under his jumper, pulled out Peter Briscoe's certificate of death, and handed it to Havis.

Havis went white as he heard Joe's awful words and read them for himself on the shocking piece of paper.

"What does this mean . . .? he stammered. "Who *is* young Mr Peter . . .?"

"That's another story," said Joe. He felt sure that Havis wouldn't tell Mr Pollard, even if he was on Pollard's side. No one would want to tell him the tragic news that his only son had died at one day old. "All Peter wants now," Joe added softly, "is to get away and find his real mum and dad. And he needs help."

Havis was stunned and didn't speak for several seconds.

"How long has Mr Peter known this?" he said at last.

"We found his mother's diary a few days ago. We started to suspect things then. I found the letter yesterday. I was showing it to Peter when Mr Woods butted in."

Havis's eyes narrowed again, and he turned his head quickly, not with his usual butler-ish calm.

Joe realised he had taken a huge risk. Would Havis suddenly laugh because he'd lured Joe into giving away his secrets? Or would he sympathise and help him to keep Pollard's men away from Peter? Joe waited an agonising few seconds. As he stared at Havis across the sill, he wondered. Had he made a new friend, or given vital information to the enemy? It was like lifting a stone and wondering whether there was a bag of gold under it, or a poisonous snake.

He waited longer, trying to read Havis's impassive features. At last the butler's head rotated slowly, and he spoke in a near-silent whisper.

"The best thing you can do, Mr Joe," he said, "is to find Peter in the village before Mr Woods does."

"How can I? I'm locked in here and I haven't got a helicopter."

"I'm afraid that my memory has been rather remiss lately, Mr Joe. Advancing age can be a terrible thing. Why – *I'll be forgetting to lock doors next*. One of these days I'll *walk* into the village. It'll slip my mind that there's a *bicycle* in the garage . . ."

It was Joe's turn to stare at Havis.

"Now think, Mr Joe. What would Mr Peter do if he couldn't get to a telephone? Where would he go?"

Joe thought carefully.

"I don't know. Anywhere he could hide, I suppose."

"But he couldn't hide for ever, Mr Joe. What would *you* do? You'd be hungry. You'd be alone. Frightened."

"He wants to find his real family. I'm sure he doesn't want anything else – not now. He wouldn't want to go home yet, and I don't think he'd go to the police, either."

"If he *did* get to a telephone, Mr Joe. Would he leave a message? Where would he leave it?"

Joe taxed his brains again.

"He certainly wouldn't phone here, and he wouldn't phone his uncle – " suddenly – "*he'd phone my mum!*"

Havis looked at Joe's bright face, slipped something out of his hip pocket and pressed it into Joe's hand.

"Honestly, Mr Joe. Mr Pollard's memory is just as bad as mine . . . He seems to have mislaid *this*!"

As Havis lifted his hand and moved away from the window to the door, Joe looked down at his own hand and the object that was lying there. It was a trim little mobile telephone.

It took Joe two minutes to escape from the house without being seen, two minutes to cross to the garages, and one minute to find the bicycle. It was a good mountain bike, and he rode it through the shrubbery to the bottom of the dusty drive, then as fast as he could along the two miles of country road that took him to the outskirts of the village. He dismounted, hid in a thick cluster of trees, and took out Mr Pollard's mobile phone.

Peter opened his eyes. He was looking at the world at grass level, and he was surprised to find that a pair of shoes were standing a few centimetres from his nose. He sat up, rubbing his eyes. Above the shoes were trousers, and above those he discovered a jacket, a shirt – and inside them all – Mr Woods.

His sleepy brain was kick-started to life, and his heart leapt up to his throat and started racing in panic.

"You didn't get very far," Mr Woods said, scornfully. He yawned, as if to prove that catching Peter had been easy.

Peter glanced round for an escape route, but found none. He couldn't believe that Mr Woods had found him. How could he? His safe hideaway had suddenly become a prison. He was surrounded by the grass cuttings, the hedge and the shed, and his only exit was blocked by Mr Woods. There didn't seem to be any way to avoid capture.

He wondered where Joe was, and what he was doing.

Mr Woods lowered his smug face towards Peter's. The hot, smelly breath of a night without sleep and no toothbrush enveloped Peter in a cloud, making him feel sick.

"So now let's have those papers," he sneered.

"What papers?" said Peter, turning away, stalling as best he could. "I don't know what you're talking about."

"Yes, you do. I saw your friend Joe give them to you. So don't muck about. You've wasted enough of everyone's time as it is. Just hand them over."

"I can't."

"There's no such word as can't."

"There is if I've hidden them."

"Oh, so you *do* know what I'm talking about? Come on – hand them over."

"I told you – I can't. I've hidden them."

"Where have you hidden them?"

"I'm not likely to tell you that, am I? There wouldn't be much point hiding them."

"You haven't hidden them. You've still got them on you."

"No I haven't. You can search me if you want."

"All right," said Mr Woods, "I will." He grabbed Peter by the wrist, and Peter let out a scream that froze the contents of Mr Woods' bloodstream. He shouted, "Help, help! *Help me! HELP! HELP*!" and started kicking Mr Woods' shins.

*

Hand shaking, Joe punched the buttons for his home telephone number. It was engaged the first time, then it was clear.

"Mum?"

"You again, Joe? What's up now? This phone's been going non-stop. First you, then Peter's uncle, then Peter, then Mr Woods, now you again."

Joe was horrified.

"Did you say *Mr Woods*?"

"Yes. I've just put the phone down now, this second. He rang Peter's uncle to get our number. Then he phoned me, asking if Peter had called. Wants to go and collect him, he said, and bring him home. I wish I knew what's going on."

Joe's horror turned to alarm.

"Did you say Peter rang as well?"

"Yes. He told me to tell you he's in the churchyard."

"You didn't tell that to Mr Woods, did you?"

"Well, yes, love, I—"

"Oh-oh! Thanks, Mum. Bye!"

Joe swivelled his horror-struck face towards the village, slapped down the cover of the telephone and pushed it into his pocket.

"*Peter's in the churchyard*," he chanted under his breath, "*and Mr Woods found out half a minute ago!*"

In two seconds he was out of the trees, and on his way towards the tower of the church that protruded above the trees a few hundred metres away.

As Peter wriggled in Mr Woods' iron grip, trying to avoid being searched, he saw a flash of metal speeding past the nearby hedge, followed by the sound of skidding rubber on loose pebbles and grass. He screamed again, and his scream merged with a different blood-congealing shriek.

It was Mr Woods' turn to be surprised.

Seconds after the alien shriek, he was hit in the small of his

135

back by a mountain bike and a thirteen-year-old boy.

Mr Woods' lungs deflated like fatally wounded balloons, and the force of the collision sent him head over heels, missing Peter, and deposited him upside down on the grass. He released his grip on Peter's wrist, and Peter found his view of Mr Woods changed magically into a view of Joe.

"Joe!"

"Come on!" shouted Joe. "Let's get out of here!"

CHAPTER FIFTEEN

Eckington Bridge

Peter leapt on to the saddle behind Joe and felt the power of Joe's legs standing on the pedals and propelling them away from their stricken enemy. He saw the church fly past to his right, and shrubbery to his left in blurs of stone and green. Out on the main road there was no traffic, and no one saw them. Peter watched as the village shop went by, followed by a few houses, before Joe turned into a side road, then left into another. They seemed to be heading towards woodland that Peter could see on the outskirts of the village. Joe chose a road that led into a track that bordered the woods, then stopped the bike.

They dismounted and ran into the dark protective shelter of the trees. They threw themselves down on the ground, Joe panting from the effort and Peter from relief. Presently they heard the sound of the helicopter thrashing across the sky not far away.

Peter was too stunned and breathless to say anything at first. He just smiled and shook his head in the fallen leaves, hardly daring to believe that once again – thanks to Joe – he had escaped Mr Woods' clutches.

"How did he find me?" he said at last.

"The same way I did," said Joe, sitting up and brushing off leaves. "You told my mum where you were, but Mr Woods found her number and she told him as well. She didn't have a clue what was going on. She thought it was all a game."

"I hope you told her it *was* a game," said Peter, worried.

Joe gave him a sideways glance.

"Of course I did. I didn't want to get her panicking and

calling the police and stuff. It was lucky I phoned only a few seconds after Mr Woods, otherwise I'd never have got to you in time."

Peter started thinking about his next move. He wanted more than anything else in the world to get to Chichester. He wanted to go to the local library and look up telephone directories and voters lists and all the things that Mr Pollard had mentioned to help him to find his family – the Harwood family.

"How long do you think we should stay here?" he said after a pause.

"I don't know," said Joe. "Mr Pollard's got his men all over the place. Cars, a helicopter. We don't stand much chance in the open, and we don't stand *any* chance unless we can get away from the village."

Mr Pollard sat at his desk furiously drumming his fingers, waiting for the phone call that would tell him that Peter had been found. Instead, the telephone rang and Woods' voice came through, sounding breathless.

"Mr Pollard . . . I nearly had Peter" – puff – "actually got my hands on him" – puff – "then his friend crashed into me with a mountain bike and" – puff – "left me winded."

"His friend? You don't mean Joe? He's still locked up here. Havis—"

"No, he ain't, Mr Pollard" – puff – "it was definitely him."

"How long ago was this?"

"Two minutes."

"Right. Contact the other cars immediately and get them to patrol all the roads out of the village. Tell the chopper as well – and when you speak to Norman, get him to ring me. Got that?"

"Yes, Mr Pollard."

He put down the phone and pressed the bell for Havis. When Havis didn't come, he leaned forward and pressed it again, harder. There was still no response. He ran to the room where Joe was supposed to have been kept, and found the door unlocked and Joe gone. Back in his office, he tried Havis's walkie-talkie, got no answer, and frowned.

Then the telephone rang and Norman came on the line.

"I'm patrolling the roads on the north side," he said. "The others are covering the rest between them. Did you want something else?"

"Yes," said Mr Pollard, still drumming. "You know the village. I want to know what they'd do if they don't try to bike out."

"They can go cross-country for miles, if they want, before they get to a road."

"We'll have to hope the chopper will cover that."

"There's woods they can hide in until it's dark."

"Get someone to help you search them after you've got the roads covered. What else?"

"They could go to someone's house and ask for a lift out."

"Not much we can do about that one – but I don't think they'd try it, do you?"

"They could call a taxi."

"They haven't got a phone, and Woods is covering the call box – unless they call at a house and ask to use one."

"They might."

"Well, there's only G-Cabs in the village. I'll talk to Gary – he owes me a favour."

"Another thing the boys could do is tell the police."

"If they were going to do that, they'd've done it by now. I don't know why they haven't – but we might be in trouble if they do."

"Or they could phone home and get one of the family to collect them. It'd take longer, but they'd probably feel safer. Which do you think they'll do?"

Mr Pollard considered.

"I think they'll lie low until dark, and then strike across

139

country. I wonder if I can borrow an infra-red camera for the chopper . . . They'd never escape if I had that . . ."

"That's all I can think of, Mr Pollard."

"Thanks, Norman. Good luck."

He kept the phone in his hand and dialled another number. "G-Cabs? Gary? This is Frank. It's just a long shot, but if any of your lads pick up one or two boys from the village, there's a hundred in it if you just tell me where they get dropped off. There's nothing shady about it – one of them's my son. Yeah! Thanks."

As soon as he put down the phone, he tried Havis's bell once more, with the same result. His suspicions about Havis were growing, so he went looking, checking every room in the house and everywhere outside. There was no doubt about it. Havis had disappeared.

"Why don't we just keep going through these woods?" said Peter. "The chopper won't be able to see us, and if we can get out into the country, the cars won't be able to find us, either."

Joe seemed to like the idea, and they agreed it was the best thing to do. They hid the bike in thick undergrowth, then set off on foot, heading away from the village, keeping as near to the centre line of the trees as they could.

As they walked, Joe told Peter how Havis had helped him to escape.

"I think he's a friend," Joe said, "but you can never be sure, really, can you?"

"Why do you think he helped you?"

Joe pondered.

"They might have sent me to find you, so they could catch us both. But I think it was me telling him that Pollard was a crook that did it. I think he doesn't like Mr Pollard and wants to help us."

At that moment their conversation was startled to an end

by a high pitched warbling sound coming from Joe's pocket. "What's that?" said Peter, alarmed.

Joe reached into his pocket, pulled out the telephone, and balanced it on his hand.

"It's my mobile telephone," said Joe.

"How long have you had that?"

"It's Mr Pollard's. Havis gave it to me."

"What?" Peter was stupefied.

"Shall I answer it?"

"If it's Mr Pollard's, it could be anyone calling. It might even be Mr Pollard trying to find his telephone."

"If it's anyone we don't know, I'll just say we're not in," said Joe, grinning.

He pressed the green button and said "Hello," making his voice as deep and gruff and as much like Mr Pollard's as he could. He relaxed as Havis's familiar tones faded and swelled across the airwaves.

"Mr Joe?"

"Yes?"

"Eckington Bridge. Twelve o'clock. Go to Eckington Bridge. I'll—"

Then the voice crackled and shrank and turned into white noise, and the line was lost. Joe hung up and waited for it to ring again, but it stayed silent.

"What did he say, Joe?"

"He said Eckington Bridge, that's all. Just Eckington Bridge. And twelve o'clock."

"Is it a place? Does he want us to be there at twelve o'clock? Is that what he means?"

"I suppose so."

"What else did he say?"

"Nothing. He was cut off."

Peter was anxious.

"It could be a trick. Are you sure it was Havis?"

"It sounded like Havis to me. And he called me *Mr* Joe."

141

"What time is it now?"

"Ten past eleven."

"That means we've got less than an hour to get there, and we don't even know where it is."

"No," said Joe. He waved the mobile in the air. "But we can find out."

Peter watched as Joe pressed buttons on the mobile until a voice crackled on the other end.

"Can you tell me the number of a taxi service in Little Haston, please?" He paused, waiting and listening. "Seven-five-five, three-one-two. Thanks."

Joe stabbed the buttons again.

"Is that G-Cabs? Could you pick up two people from the road that leads to the woods, and take them to . . . I'll tell him when he gets here. In ten minutes? Thanks."

"I hope you've got some money," said Peter. "I'm broke."

"I've got enough," said Joe.

Peter followed Joe as they started walking back the way they had come, and began to feel more and more worried as they neared civilisation again. They showed extreme caution as they approached the road, but when they saw the taxi waiting, with the sign "G-Cabs" on the roof, they felt safe. They ran from the trees and ducked into the car.

"How far is it to Eckington Bridge?" said Joe. "And how much will it cost?"

"It's about nine miles," said the driver, who sounded friendly, "and it won't cost you more than a week's pocket-money."

"Can you take us, then, please?"

Peter and Joe lay down on the back seat, out of sight, and the car set off. The driver didn't seem to think it unusual for his clients to lie on the back seat, and said nothing about it. In hardly any time at all, he was pointing up ahead.

"See the traffic lights?" He waited for their heads to come up. "That's Eckington Bridge."

The light was green and there was no traffic behind them. Joe paid the driver, and they walked on to the narrow span, pausing to look up and down the wide river Avon that flowed gently through the red stone arches beneath them. The taxi drove off, with the driver talking on his intercom.

"That's downstream," said Joe. He pointed to their right, away from the car park that lay on the far side.

They lazed on the grass in the warm sunshine to rest, but Peter was still nervous.

"What happens now?" he said.

"Don't know," said Joe. "Havis just said Eckington Bridge and twelve o'clock, that's all."

"Do you think he'll meet us?"

"I don't know any more than you."

"You do. You spoke to him at the house. Did he look as if he was going to help us?"

"He did help us. He gave us the mobile phone."

"It's twenty to twelve," said Peter. "I think we ought to hide, in case it's a trap."

They hid in a clump of bushes and waited as the time passed achingly slowly. Twelve minutes later a Rolls Royce crept towards the bridge and waited at the red light, but neither of them was looking in that direction. The light changed to green and the Rolls passed across to the other side. It was only when it stopped, almost blocking the far entrance to the bridge, that Peter and Joe realised who it was.

"It's Norman!" they squawked simultaneously, then both leapt to their feet, looking this way and that for the best means of escape.

Moments later, a light green sports car came from behind them, with Mr Woods and another man inside. It was followed closely by a Porsche containing Mr Pollard and two more men. Norman was already out of the Rolls and walking towards them. The other two cars screeched to a halt near the bridge and the five men leapt out.

Peter and Joe hadn't waited to be found and boxed in near the bridge, and were already a hundred metres along the northern bank of the river, going west.

The six men raced off along the riverside, pursuing the flying blobs of Peter and Joe.

Peter and Joe ran through the long grass in the meadow that bordered the river, wishing it was a proper footpath, and glanced back to see who was chasing them.

One of the men had stopped to examine his shoes, Mr Woods was slowing down and trying to loosen his clothing, and Norman and two other men were already down to a jog. But Mr Pollard was overtaking them all, shouting them on, and was now within forty or fifty metres of Peter and Joe.

"There are six of them!" panted Joe.

Peter didn't answer, but put on an extra spurt.

Suddenly, they realised there was a wide stream ahead of them, winding its way out of the meadow and severing their path where it flowed into the Avon.

Joe's voice shrieked through the air that blew into Peter's face.

"Swim! Swim!"

Peter and Joe were almost up to the tributary that interrupted their progress, and all the time Mr Pollard was gaining on them. Peter didn't need any further prompting.

The Avon was wide, but slow. There was a boat coming upstream, not very far away, but far enough for safety. Peter didn't stop running, changed direction by a few degrees, and took a racing dive through the reeds into the river. Joe followed close behind. As soon as they hit the cold water most of the remaining breath was knocked out of their lungs. They both swam a weak breast-stroke, gasping for air, making slow progress towards the opposite bank.

Mr Pollard kicked off his shoes, losing precious seconds, threw down his wallet, and dived in after them. Peter and

Joe were only halfway across, still struggling, and the boat was getting nearer and nearer. Mr Pollard was gaining on them as well. With ten determined strokes, he had almost caught them.

The boat was only fifty metres away now, and it wasn't slowing down. Perhaps it hadn't seen them.

"Stop!" spluttered Peter.

They could see the pilot, a tall figure in dark glasses, hair blowing in the wind, a determined grimace on his lips.

"Stop!" Both of them shouted this time, waving their arms. "Stop!"

They might as well have been dumb and invisible.

They heard the frightening change in the cruiser's engine note and watched in horror as the figure in dark glasses piled on more power and headed straight towards Peter and Joe in the water.

CHAPTER SIXTEEN

Journey's End

Forty metres, thirty, twenty. The boat bore down on Peter and Joe, closer and closer. Mr Pollard had turned in the water and was trying to swim clear, and everyone on the bank and on the boat was shouting and screaming and waving arms in all directions.

The boat's engine suddenly fell to nothing and roared again as it was almost upon them. The water at its stern seemed to boil, and the little dinghy it had in tow bobbed wildly on the froth and swung out sideways. The cruiser had gone into reverse. It came to a standstill, separating the struggling boys on one side and Mr Pollard on the other.

Then another figure appeared on the boat, tall and elderly, carrying a boat-hook. He shouted down to the boys in the water.

"*Into the dinghy, Mr Peter! Into the dinghy, Mr Joe!*"

"Havis!" they both spluttered together.

In the same moment, Mr Pollard heard the instruction and struck out for the dinghy himself. With half a dozen powerful strokes he almost reached it. Havis leaned over the side, inserted a boat-hook into the belt of his employer's trousers, and gently pushed him under the water.

On the other side, the breathless boys dragged themselves into the little boat and lay there, exhausted. The cruiser's engine roared again as the pilot turned it to face downstream, and as soon as it was safely under way with Peter and Joe in the dinghy behind, Havis released the trouser-belt and watched his boss come spluttering to the surface in the middle of the river.

Above the chug of the engine they heard a water-logged, gruff, angry voice gasping in the boat's choppy wake.

"Havis! You're sacked!"

From the boat, already twenty metres away, the mild, creaking voice of his ex-butler floated over the water.

"Thank you, sir!" it said.

Mr Pollard's dripping form was then pulled from the river by his henchmen. His final words drifted towards them on the gentle breeze.

"Back to the cars! We'll get them at Strensham Lock!"

A little further downstream, the cruiser passed under a railway bridge, then pulled into the bank. Joe and Peter had recovered slightly, and were given a helping hand to transfer from the dinghy to the boat. They were wrapped in big blankets to keep them warm, and the little party set off again. The engine of the cruiser throbbed and bubbled as it made its way hastily down the river.

"Thanks, Havis, thanks a million!" breathed Peter.

"I thought we'd had it!" said Joe.

"Sorry about that," said the pilot. "I had to speed up to cut you off from Pollard. If he'd managed to grab you, we'd have had a real problem."

Havis introduced the pilot as an old friend of his, Mr Clark.

"I thought it would be easy to get you down river without being discovered," Havis explained. "But Mr Pollard obviously found you first. And I'm afraid we're not in the clear. It sounds from his comments as if he may be planning a rendezvous at Strensham Lock, and I don't see how we can avoid him."

"Can't we just turn round and go back to Eckington?" said Peter, tightening the blanket round himself.

"It's a possibility, Mr Peter," said Havis.

"He might leave some of his men there, as well," said Joe.

"That is also a possibility," agreed Havis.

147

"I think we should just carry on," said Peter.

"I've an idea," said Mr Clark. He pointed. "Hand me that map over there."

Joe, still in his blanket, dived for the map. He opened it out, and Mr Clark stuck a big, square finger on it in between Eckington and the M5 motorway.

"I can set you down there," he said. Three pairs of eyes crowded together to follow his fingernail, which indicated a little track with a few houses next to the river. "It's only a mile from there to the M5 services at Strensham – with a little bit of fence-hopping. You can hire a car there, and go wherever you want. It's round the bend out of sight of Strensham Lock, so even if they're watching for us, they won't see us. Even if they knew you were going to the M5 services, it's more than ten miles by road. And you'd better make your minds up, because we're coming to it soon."

This time the big finger pointed ahead on the right side of the river.

"I think that's what we should do," Havis decided. "It's too dangerous to take our chances at the lock."

Everyone agreed, and the boat chugged on in the thin autumn sunshine.

"I'm sorry you've lost your job for my sake," said Peter.

"I already had suspicions about Mr Pollard's activities," Havis shrugged. "I didn't like it when he told me to lock up Mr Joe, so it was just the catalyst I needed to resign."

"It was very kind of you to arrange the boat to rescue us."

"Think nothing of it, Mr Peter."

Peter lay on the top of the boat and closed his eyes for a last few minutes of peace and freedom. He felt the throb of the engine beating through his body like a massage. A boat passed in the opposite direction. Peter sat up and waved, and they all waved back.

"Off season," said Mr Clark. "Not many boats about this time of year."

As the fields and banks slipped by, Peter lay down again and turned his face towards the weak sunshine. It was the first time he'd been on a big boat on a river. He loved the gentle motion and the light breeze, and the ducks scurrying from the bows, quacking. He drifted into sleep for a few minutes and woke when his ears picked out a tiny sound that he couldn't understand. It came into his head like a distant lark singing in the sky, but as the seconds ticked by it became more human. He wondered if it was the voice, but for once he didn't know.

They soon reached the bank where the houses were. Mr Clark tied up the boat, and he and Havis shared a hushed conversation while Peter and Joe unloaded themselves on to the meadow-side. Then Havis led them across the meadow, and through a gate that emerged into a dusty lane near a few houses. At the top of the lane, they turned left.

At Strensham services they hired two cars. Havis explained carefully to Peter that he needed Joe's help, which meant separating the two boys. Joe would go with Havis in one car, and Peter would go with Mr Clark in the other. With a promise that they would meet the following day, Joe and Peter sped off in separate directions.

Peter had no idea why Havis needed Joe, and he couldn't begin to guess. Havis had refused to say anything further on the subject. Mr Clark went first to some shops and bought Peter dry underclothes, jeans, jumper, socks and trainers. Peter rescued the envelope with its precious contents, and laid them out on the car seat at the back to dry. The ink in the letter had run a little, and everything was wrinkled, but legible.

He fell asleep in the car soon afterwards, and when he woke up they had arrived in Gloucester.

Mr Clark took Peter to a semi-detached house on the outskirts of the city and introduced him to Havis's young niece and her husband. They had a son called Derek, who was ten and not very communicative, and Peter was too tired to contribute very much. They spent most of the evening watching television.

Peter did some thinking while the flashing screen droned on, and decided to write some letters. His new friends supplied pen and paper, which he took to Derek's bedroom, and began. First, he wrote a long letter to Mr Pollard.

Dear Mr Pollard,

Thank you very much for inviting me to your house and letting Joe come as well. We really enjoyed the Rolls Royce. I am very sorry to tell you that I am not your son. It makes me sad to tell you that your son Peter died when he was only one day old. It says so in his mother's diary. I am also sorry to say that Deirdre Briscoe was not my mother, either. When she lost Peter she snatched me from my pram and that's the main reason why she had to run so far away and change her name. I am going back home now to my real family. I hope I can find them.

I know you want the letter badly, but I have decided to keep it somewhere safe. It was very wrong of you to burgle my uncle's house looking for it. I think you should go and see him and tell him you're sorry and do something to make up for it.

I hope you'll be a better person from now on, and use your bad money to help others instead of yourself. If I hear of you doing good things, I might give you back the letter one day. But I shall always keep the code, and hide it where no one can ever find it.

Yours sincerely, James [Peter Briscoe].

Next, he wrote to his uncle.

Dear Uncle,

I know this will come as a big shock, but I am not the real

Peter Briscoe. Joe and I found a diary in the attic saying that your nephew Peter died when he was only one day old. We found the death certificate as well, so it's true. Mum (Deirdre) snatched me from a pram the next day. I know now who I am, and I am going to find my real family.

I know that you have used the money that Mum left me to buy your car and start your business, and I suppose you thought you might pay it back one day. But Mum left the money to her son, Peter, who's dead, so I suppose you would have it now, anyway. What I'm saying is, I want you to keep it.

I'll come and see you as soon as I can,
Yours, James [Peter Briscoe]."

He decided not to mention the letter or the coded message.

Later that evening he had a quiet game of cards with Derek, and at ten o'clock it was lights out. They whispered for a while until Derek grunted and went quiet.

Another hour passed and Peter couldn't sleep. With a shock he suddenly realised that the next day was his birthday. He'd be thirteen. Uncle Len wouldn't give him a present now, not after running away – no one would. Even Mr Pollard might have bought him something, but he wouldn't give it to him now – especially when he received Peter's letter. And Joe. Joe would probably forget as well.

The sound of the television downstairs faded, and he heard Derek's parents creeping up the stairs and going to bed. Now he could only hear the gentle rhythm of Derek's breathing on the bed nearby, and the occasional passing car.

At last, when everything was silent, the voice came into his head again. It wasn't speaking English, or any language. It wasn't even speaking. He couldn't explain. It was just there, probing, tugging at his mind like someone poking with a stick. It was calling his name, but it wasn't Peter.

James!

151

It was calling James! The shock was so sudden that Peter sat up in the darkness and listened. Had someone called James? Was it in his head or was it just somebody in the street outside? He strained his ears, listening. Nothing. He lay down again, his pulse drumming. And when his heart was still and all was silent, it came again. In his head. Calling. Calling him.

James! *James*!

Peter concentrated his mind.

I'm here! he tried to say, but it seemed to evaporate in the darkness. *I'm here*!

James! *James*!

Yes, I'm here! It's me! I'm coming! I'm coming soon!

Gradually, he became more and more tired, so tired that even the excitement couldn't keep him awake. The voice in his head grew tired, too, and he heard the clock downstairs strike one. By the time it struck the quarter he was asleep.

In the morning, Derek shook him awake and gave him a cup of tea. Peter smiled and thanked him.

"Uncle Henry just phoned," Derek announced. "He's collecting you at two o'clock."

"Good old Havis!" said Peter. "He's been fantastic!"

"He's funny sometimes, though. He wanted to know what you're wearing."

"Who, Havis?"

"Yes – Uncle Henry. He said 'Did Mr Clark buy new things for Peter?' and I said 'Yes', and he said 'What were they?' and I said 'Jeans and jumper and trainers'."

"That's odd," said Peter.

"And then he said 'What colour?' and I said blue jeans and green jumper' and he said 'What sort of green?' and I had to try and explain what sort of green over the telephone."

Peter was intrigued.

"Why on earth would he want to know what I'm wearing?"

he said, mystified.

"My uncle's a bit mad like that sometimes."

"But why would he want to know what *colour*?"

"Perhaps he's forgotten what you look like," said Derek. It was the first time Peter had heard him make a joke.

After this exchange, Peter slipped into the bathroom and carried out the basic essentials, then dressed and hurried down the stairs. He had an enormous cooked breakfast, including fruit juice and cereal and toast. Afterwards, rather than feeling full, he felt refreshed and excited. It was his birthday, and for the first time in his life, no one knew. It didn't matter. It was like a lovely secret.

He was going home – home to a new home – and he couldn't think of anything better than that for a birthday present. He'd lost his mother, but he still had Joe and a grumpy uncle, and now there was a chance of being part of another family. He wondered if he'd like them.

He went with Derek to post his letters, then back to the house. The morning seemed to last a lifetime. What was Havis doing? If he was trying to find his real mother and father, why had he needed Joe? How would he find his family, anyway? Even if there was an address, they probably would have moved years ago, and no one would know where they'd gone. That's usually what happened if people moved away.

They spent the morning playing card games (Derek didn't have a computer) and then had another enormous meal to make up for the ones Peter had missed since running away.

At two o'clock the doorbell rang, and Peter and Derek and his parents all rushed to the front door together.

"Havis!"

"Good afternoon, Mr Peter, sir."

"Joe!"

"Hi!"

There was a lot of hand-shaking and hello-ing, and Peter

found it difficult to stop grinning. They exchanged brief bits of news, then thanked Derek's parents and Derek for all they had done, and bade them farewell.

Peter climbed in the front of the car, with Joe in the back, and Havis drove them away.

"Are you taking me to Chichester now?" Peter asked.

"No, sir."

Peter's face fell as he was gripped with a horrible fear.

"You're not taking me back home, are you?"

"No, sir."

Another of Peter's nightmares came to the surface – the one where he discovered that Havis was really on Mr Pollard's side.

"Not to Mr Pollard's?"

"Of course not, sir."

"Have you seen him again since the river?"

"No, sir. But I understand he is currently entertaining a visit from the police. The Inland Revenue have also asked for an appointment, and so have Her Majesty's Customs and Excise."

"Really?" said Peter, smiling. "What happened?"

"I gave them some of his files, sir."

Peter absorbed the information for a moment in silence.

"Does that mean he'll go to prison?"

"I think it's highly likely, sir."

Peter felt glad.

"Well if we're not going home, and we're not going to Chichester, where *are* we going, Havis?"

"To Winchester, sir."

"Winchester? Why Winchester?"

"Would you like to show him, Mr Joe?"

Joe's hand shot across Peter's shoulder, holding out a piece of paper. Peter took it and read.

"*Mr and Mrs Harwood, 14 Park Way, Winchester, Hampshire.*"

Peter, who had vowed never to cry again, felt an uncomfortable lump rising in his throat and his eyes going misty. He swallowed and blinked, trying not to give himself away.

"Is that them?" he said, but his voice came out in a croak and he felt the top of his nose tightening up.

"Yes," said Joe.

Peter swallowed and his voice returned more or less to normal.

"How do you know?"

"We phoned 'em."

"*They know I'm coming?*"

"Of course they do. They've lived abroad for the last eight years. They only came back a few months ago."

Peter's thoughts went flying all over the place, and he didn't know what to say next.

"Shall I tell him the other bit?" said Joe, to Havis.

"Sir?"

"About the newspaper cutting, and the corner that the mouse had eaten . . .?"

"Oh, no, Mr Joe. That would spoil the surprise."

"What do you mean – the missing bit?" Peter turned his head to look at Joe, and Joe was grinning.

"You saw the newspaper. There's a corner missing . . ."

"Oh, sir . . ." interrupted Havis, frowning.

"Well," Joe went on relentlessly, "we thought it said '*Young* Baby Snatched Outside Grocer's . . .' "

"What did it say, then?"

"I really don't think, Mr Joe . . ."

"We looked it up in the newspaper archives this morning . . ."

"And what did it *say*?"

Joe grinned again.

"You'll have to wait and see, won't you?"

"Joe!"

Joe started laughing his head off, and Havis smiled at him and heaved a sigh of relief. Peter hammered Joe's knees, but couldn't get him to say another word.

"You rat!" he said.

Then Havis said, teasing, "I think the green jumper's about the right shade, don't you, Mr Joe?"

Joe, smirking in the back, agreed that it was.

"The right shade for *what*?" screamed Peter. He knew he was being teased, but neither Joe nor Havis would give him any more clues.

The car buzzed along. Cirencester, Swindon, Newbury. Places that Peter had heard of, but never seen in his life before. Trees and houses flashed by at seventy miles an hour, and every minute made him more and more nervous. What if he didn't like his new family? What if they didn't like him? What if his uncle made a fuss and wanted him back just to be spiteful? What if Mr Pollard started making a fuss?

Down the dual carriageway to Winchester. Into the town. Down a few side streets. They reached the house – a semi-detached house overlooking fields at the back.

Peter felt his nerves cracking up.

And the voice was back in his brain. Here! Here!

Was he going completely mad?

They led him up the steps, Joe and Havis saying things, but he couldn't hear their voices. Shapes grew in front of his eyes. There was the distant ringing of a doorbell, but it was just there, in front of him. The door opened. Strangers, smiling, laughing, leading him into the sitting-room. Joe and Havis there with him. Strangers . . . all laughing and clapping.

Peter couldn't help it any more. The tears streamed down his cheeks as he embraced his new mother, his new father, his new big brother.

But still the voice was calling.

They all started to sing "Happy Birthday!" and they heaped him with more presents than he'd ever had in his life before. Big presents from Havis and Joe, huge presents from his new parents, and his brother.

They told him that his real birthday had gone, a week ago.

Then, from behind the crowd, saving himself till last, stepped a boy. A thirteen-year-old boy. The same age as him. Tears in those eyes, too. Blue jeans just like his. A green jumper, just the same shade as his. And a face – a face just like his. A mirror image of Peter. *The voice*.

At the same moment, Joe held a newspaper cutting in front of Peter's eyes, grinning.

Through the mist, Peter saw the headline, "*Twin* Baby Snatched Outside Grocer's," as he embraced his long-lost twin brother.

Did you enjoy *Skeletons in the Attic*?
If you would like to know what happens to the secret papers,
read the fifth book in David Schutte's Naitabal mystery
series, *Ghost Island*.

1. DANGER, KEEP OUT!
ISBN 1-904028-00-4   £5.00

Miss Coates steamed up the garden path. Her white hair glowed in the moonlight. She stopped at the well in the middle of her lawn, and shone her torch into it. And then . . . she disappeared.

To ordinary people, she's Miss Coates, but to the Naitabals she's the old enemy battleship, the SS *Coates*. And she's hiding something. Why has she grown huge hedges around her garden, so no one can see into it? And why is she so desperate to stop anyone snooping?

Determined to discover the truth, the Naitabals go investigating. But the secrets they uncover lie deep in the past – a past that Miss Coates will do anything to conceal. . .

"Get ready for an invasion of wild ten-year-olds... "

The Daily Telegraph

2. WAKE UP, IT'S MIDNIGHT!
ISBN 1-904028-01-2   £5.00

Charlotte stood, hand poised on the doorknob, and took a deep breath. The ghostly sound of typing stopped abruptly, as suddenly as it had begun. She threw open the door. A piece of paper in the old typewriter fluttered in the moving air. But there was no one there.

The Mysterious Motionless Mr Maynard hasn't moved for two days. Beneath that hairless head and ferocious scowl, his evil brain is plotting – but plotting what?

A secret drawer, an empty house at midnight, a missing manuscript, spying, cheating – and a mysterious lady in black – are just a few of the obstacles the Naitabals must overcome to solve the mystery. Wake up, it's midnight! Join the Naitabals in their second breathtaking adventure!

"The type of story that would appeal to juniors who like reading about children outwitting the adults. . . who dream of having a tree-house and outdoor adventures, and who like codes and secret letters. It is all very entertaining. . ."

Junior Bookshelf

More Naitabal Mysteries by David Schutte

3. WILD WOODS, DARK SECRET
ISBN 1-904028-02-0 £5.00

The woman was moving along a track a little way above them. Instead of walking, she seemed to be sailing effortlessly, floating like a ghost above the ground...

The Naitabal gang are promised the holiday of a lifetime at Mr Blake's remote country house. But from the very first moment, their visit is plunged into mystery.

Why has Mr Blake disappeared? What is the meaning of the weird coded messages? Who are the sinister strangers that prowl the dark, forbidding woods?

Only one thing is clear – Mr Blake is in big trouble...

"The Naitabals are a wild species of human aged about 10 who inhabit these great books... I hope David Schutte can keep adding to the series..."
                                                                The School Librarian

4. BEHIND LOCKED DOORS
ISBN 1-904028-03-9 £5.00

The message was written in purple ink on yellow paper. In an almost illegible spidery scrawl, it said...
'PLEASE HELP ME!'

Mrs Hooper has not left her home or spoken to anyone for twenty years, ever since her husband died. His hat, coat and umbrella still hang in the hall, untouched, covered in dust.

Now the Naitabals realise she might be in trouble. What sinister secrets are hidden within Mrs Hooper's spooky old house? Why has she locked herself away for so long? When the Naitabals finally open the locked doors, they find a mystery far more evil than any of them could have imagined...

"Have you got a Naitabal in your garden? According to author David Schutte, a Naitabal is 'a wild species of human aged about ten', it feeds on 'anything, except what its parents want it to' and it lives mainly in tree-houses. If your own Naitabal hankers for... adventure, buy it one of Schutte's Naitabal Mysteries."
                                                                The Times

More Naitabal Mysteries by David Schutte

5. GHOST ISLAND
ISBN 1-904028-05-5   £5.00

The house that was Ghost Island was silhouetted against the sky, towering above the lake. Thick, round wooden posts stuck up out of the water a few metres from it, like giant hippo teeth, encircling the whole house as far as their eyes could see.

When the Naitabals see the unusual advertisement in their local newspaper, they know they won't rest until they can unravel its strange meaning:

```
He/she who solves this
    exquisite puzzle
should use the digits below
   to check if it fits.
        186945
```

Its solution leads them to Ghost Island – and to a mystery that has remained unsolved for fourteen years.

It's the Naitabals' biggest challenge yet.

6. DEAD MAN'S CHEST
ISBN 1-904028-06-3   £5.00

It was a light oak box strengthened with metal straps like a pirate's treasure chest. The edges of the lid were decorated with silhouettes of pirate figures burnt into the wood. Charlotte read the message branded on the lid across the middle: 'SARAH'S LITTLE TREASURE'.

The Naitabals have never seen a living soul at the lonely Deep Shadow Cottage in Gray's Wood. But when Jayne catches a glimpse of a face at the window, it heralds a chain of events that plunge even the woods themselves into danger.

Who really owns the cottage? How did a burning house link its tenant with a past cloaked in mystery?

The fifteen pirates burnt into the lid of the dead man's little wooden chest are just one of the clues that lead the Naitabals to the stunning secret.

"If your own Naitabal hankers for. . . adventure, buy it one of Schutte's Naitabal Mysteries."

The Times

Junior Genius